Praise for World's Best Mother

"This sincere and visceral chronicle
very revealing."
El País

"In *World's Best Mother*, Nuria Labari has summoned all
of the vitality and tenderness of women who have come
before and those who will come after. Rage and desire and
love and insolence—she's laid it at our feet with a wry smile,
unapologetic. It is fearless, profound and destabilizing, in
the way the best literature is."
MEAGHAN O'CONNELL, author of *And Now We Have Everything*

"Prepare to read a book like you've never read before,
one that breaks the bounds of the narrative and the
biographical, the conventions of both traditional and
alternative values. A book of humor, love, and pain; as
intoxicating as strong wine and as tumultuous as life.
The truth is that I can't imagine the possibility of
someone not liking it."
ROSA MONTERO

"An honest, deep, and visceral reflection on being a mother."
PILAR QUINTANA, author of National Book Award finalist *The Bitch*

"Labari's searing, insightful voice lights up the landscape
of reproductive biology, culture, and history, giving us
new ways to think about creativity itself. A brilliant, vital,
necessary contribution to the canon."
ELISA ALBERT, author of *After Birth*

"A story told from the edge of a knife, a fictionalized chronicle that investigates pain and darkness, but also love, solidarity, and hope."
TodoLiteratura

"In clean, quick, and pointed prose that gets into the reader's soul from the start, Labari's novel leaves space for reflections on pain and makes room for understanding and coming to the aid of the fragile, incidental individual in today's society."
El Confidencial

"Nuria sheds a light on this chaos of darkness that I inhabit when I think about my motherhood (or non-motherhood)."
PAULA BONET

"Nuria Labari shows that living motherhood and writing about it is the new punk. A book against social conventions and against the predictable."
SERGIO DEL MOLINO

"There are many ways to talk about motherhood, but Nuria Labari's book is profoundly original and brilliant. This novel is an explosion, an intellectual journey through the most primary instincts and the most human love. Nuria Labari has written a necessary book on a universal theme."
LARA MORENO, author

"Labari infuses this story with some of her own experience, going beyond the life of a protagonist who lifts the veil on stereotypes and turning this text into a universal story about motherhood loaded with humanity, doubts, humor, regrets and imperfections."
El Diario

"This novel joins the debate already opened by public figures such as Samanta Villar: the ambivalence generated by motherhood in contemporary female identity."
ANABEL PALOMARES, *Jared*

"For Labari, the important thing is to take the issue of motherhood to the streets and to books, to take away that sense of duty to be maternal that floods us and infiltrates our way of living sex."
PAOLA ARAGÓN, *Fashion & Arts*

"Nuria Labari's book must be read slowly, with a pencil, underlining. And, at the end of each chapter, get up, walk, think. It is both a necessary and insufficient book: we need more women, we need more mothers, more non-mothers, more workers, more artists, more grandmothers, more cleaners, more executives, more single mothers ... We need more voices. That said: how well you think and what a pleasure to read you, Labari. Somebody take care of those girls for a while, please. Let Nuria keep writing."
PALOMA BRAVO, *Zenda*

World's Best Mother

Motherhood, Ambivalence, Writing, Ambition, Infertility, History,
Sexuality, Love, Abortion, Philosophy, Marriage, Infidelity

Nuria Labari

World's Best Mother

Motherhood, Ambivalence, Writing, Ambition, Infertility, History,
Sexuality, Love, Abortion, Philosophy, Marriage, Infidelity

Translated from the Spanish
by Katie Whittemore

WORLD EDITIONS
New York, London, Amsterdam

Published in the USA in 2021 by World Editions LLC, New York
Published in the UK in 2021 by World Editions Ltd., London

World Editions
New York | London | Amsterdam

Printed by Lake Book, USA

The quote on page 24 is from the Bible, New Revised Standard Version, Genesis 3. The quotes on pages 28–29 are from *The Trial* by Franz Kafka, translation by Idris Parry, copyright 1994 by Penguin Random House, pp. 170–172. The quote on page 39 is from *The Divine Comedy* by Dante, *The Inferno: The Definitive Illustrated Edition*, translation by Henry Wadsworth Longfellow, copyright 2016 by Dover Publications, canto II, verses 70–73. The quote on page 41 is from the Bible, New Revised Standard Version, Genesis 28. The quote on pages 114–115 is from "Elegy 1" by Rilke, accessed from https://www.poemhunter.com/poem/elegy-i/.

Library of Congress Cataloging in Publication Data is available

ISBN 978-1-64286-072-6

First published as *La mejor madre del mundo* in Spain in 2019 by Literatura Random House, Barcelona.
This edition is published by arrangement with International Editors' Co. Literary Agency.

Support for the translation of this book was provided by Acción Cultural Española, AC/E.

ACCIÓN CULTURAL
ESPAÑOLA

Twitter: @WorldEdBooks
Facebook: @WorldEditionsInternationalPublishing
Instagram: @WorldEdBooks
www.worldeditions.org

Book Club Discussion Guides are available on our website.

For Esther Gómez Echaide, mother

ONE

The Punctuality of Playmobil Bunnies

I'm a woman, I'm a mother, I can't have children, I write. I can't have children, I'm a mother, I write, I'm a woman. I write, I'm a mother, I'm a woman, I can't have children.

I like watching the sparrows that sit on the high-tension wire outside my office in the outskirts of Madrid. They perch, equidistant, on the black line. Notes on a staff of music in the sky. I recently learned that birds position themselves like this because it's their way of being together, evenly spaced at the minimum distance between members of their species. Sometimes, when a bird tires of being with the others, it flies away. That's being a bird.

I'm a woman, not a bird. And some evenings, just before I dissolve into the traffic jam that will carry me home, I try to determine the minimum distance I should maintain with respect to other members of my own species. Some days—today, for example—I wonder if such a distance even exists. To be honest, all my points of reference were blown sky high when I became a mother. Everything's up in the air now. Everything except me. Because, unlike birds, I can't fly.

"They're doing the tests tomorrow," I said to MyMother.

Five years ago. The brief flash of her scared-squirrel face.

"I don't understand what they can tell you from a blood test. I know you think I'm very old-fashioned, but this is something new, all the stuff you girls go through these days. I never wanted to have children. I mean, not like people want them nowadays. I got pregnant without realizing it. I didn't plan, I didn't try. Of course, I was younger than you are—twenty-four. Can you imagine? You wouldn't have been an only child if your father hadn't died, that's for sure. It's different now. My gynecologist told me that you're not actually very young at thirty-five, that the reason you're not getting pregnant is because you waited too long. But it's your *insistence* that I don't understand. Babies come when they come, and if you start planning on them, they don't. I certainly wouldn't have had you, if I'd stopped to think about it. No, listen. One day, I showered to go out with your aunts, and when I went to put on my green dress with the buttons, it didn't fit. I thought it had shrunk. It didn't even occur to me to think that I'd gained weight. But I was pregnant. And I didn't stop gaining, more than fifty-five pounds in the end. After I had you, I never weighed less than 130."

"I'll get the results in ten days."

"Me! Who never weighed more than 110 pounds and had to eat cornstarch to put on weight!"

I recall many conversations that I had with MyMother when I was trying to get pregnant, all of them immaterial. Talking to one's own mother is impossible because mothers are like mute magpies: they never shut up, but they don't have anything to say. MyMother doesn't stop, words gush from her. The same messages day after day, year after year. The same stories. Her chatter, a music aimed at the back of my head. Like a revolver. And yet, it's a kind of comfort, too: when I talk to her, I'm not looking for dialogue or ideas, but the hum, her melody. Sometimes I just want the sound of her voice saying whatever it has to say, and what I have surely heard before. It used to drive me crazy. I wanted her to be direct. I thought her ideas didn't make sense, that she could do better. But now, I think it's because she's MyMother, a mother, and that means she knows her music is all I'll have left when she dies. She doesn't want to leave me alone. The medium is the message and the mothers of the world decided a long time ago that it had all been said before. No one ever listened to them, anyway. The thing is, four years ago I too became a mother. And what's worse is I still haven't found my own melody. That's why we're here, in this book that will be my failure and disappearance as a mother and as a writer, when I haven't established myself in either field.

I'm an amateur mother and I'm already done for. I write behind my daughters' backs, like they aren't enough. I write when I should be playing with them or telling them a story or making a cake. And when this book is finished they will know.

But I'm not really what you'd call a writer, either. I've written a few dozen short stories—one of them won a local prize—a novel I haven't managed to get published and another I haven't managed to finish. I make money as a creative director in a digital marketing agency. I'm good at it, they pay me well, and I enjoy myself. I have no excuse for spending my child-rearing days writing, and much less writing about motherhood, which will be the definitive confirmation of my lack of literary ambition. Because I don't think you can be an artist and write as a mother.

Talented artists are daughters, always their mothers' daughters regardless of whether or not they have their own offspring. Good writers write about *daughterhood*, or about any other subject in which their point of view forms the center of the universe. Like Vivian Gornick's

Fierce Attachments, an autopsy of motherhood in which she is the daughter, of course, because Gornick is a creator. In contrast, a mother is always the satellite of another more important body. A mother is the antithesis of the creative Ego. "Mothers do not write, they are written," pronounced the psychoanalyst Helene Deutsch around 1880. Arguably, this still stands today.

That's how I know that if I persist in this, I'll end up strolling into publishers' offices with a manuscript under my arm that will sooner or later be labeled "a woman's intimate journal," an invisible category that, in book circles, denotes a highly suspect lack of literary ambition.

I read enough to know that any text that smacks of the female experience is to literature what tampons are to the big drugstores: a "feminine hygiene" product. In Europe, you can buy Tampax in the same places you buy expensive perfume, but each product sits on its own shelf and every shelf has its value.

The masculine experience, by contrast, has always invoked universal themes. There are no "typically male subjects" because for centuries boys' themes belonged to everyone. At least that's what I notice whenever I've poked around in the intimate experience of a man I'm close to. But the reverse doesn't happen often. The male experience is all of ours, while the female experience belongs to women alone.

This subtle poison of prejudice is perceived throughout literary history. Sometimes I think about how if Kafka's *Letter to His Father* had been a *Letter to His Mother*, it would have been considered the clucking of a hen and not a rooster's proud crow. We've accepted that some are destined to wake the very sun with their morning call while the rest of us limit ourselves to pecking at the ground and laying eggs.

If that weren't enough, there is a silent—and silencing—battle between what it means to create as a mother and to create as a woman. There are three unwritten rules: a woman's most important creation will be her children, motherhood her greatest achievement, and, for as long as she lives, her children will be her greatest passion. This is why I think there are so many more mothers who write than there is writing by mothers: we almost always prefer to use what we create to connect with the other *I* that we are able to be when we aren't raising children. Out of my way for a moment, child, I'm going to write, I'm going to dance, I'm going to act, I'm going to paint. I read authors (mothers) who talk about writing as "their space." And they write an article or a few stories about motherhood, or poems, lots of poems, entire books of poems, sometimes. In writing about motherhood, it seems you must betray either yourself or your child, or maybe both, as in my case. There is only one way that the experience of motherhood becomes universal, and that's the death of a child. At that point, you just have to dig in, because there's no other way to go on, if one can somehow go on. The creator's point of view (her pain) is once again the center of the universe.

In *The Year of Magical Thinking*, Joan Didion approaches the theme of motherhood (among others) after her husband's death and the serious illness of her daughter, who would die shortly after the book was published and about whom she would write in *Blue Nights*. Her autofiction is a contemporary classic; it's not relegated to the tampon shelf. Maybe tragedy is the only way to turn motherhood into a universal theme. Maybe without pain, there are no universal themes. Maybe without pain, there is no universe.

And so, in general, great women writers focus on *their*

writing in addition to *their children* (when they have them). Two circus rings. Two types of music, two dances. This is the best-case scenario, of course, when the mother-artist divides herself between raising children and creating. The problem is that I'm not even a writer, and I haven't suffered any misfortune that legitimizes my need to write about motherhood. My responsibility—without a doubt—is to take care of my daughters and keep quiet. Because nothing hurts. Because everything is fine, really. The girls are fine, Man is fine, work is fine. We are healthy enough, have enough money. But here I am, holed up in a café, far from them, writing, when I know this is bad for them, I know that the three of us would be better off if I went home and we hid out in the bottom bunk. If we started to play Playmobil zoo, baby edition, and I made a cave with the comforter to protect us from a pretend storm. And set up the fences for the jungle beasts and the pens for the farm animals. It must be time to feed the Playmobil bunnies right about now. They're always terribly punctual.

A writing mother is a guilty mother. And a guilty book chokes, in the end: another manuscript shoved in a drawer.

An important female editor gave me some advice when I told her I was working on this book. "If you're going to write about motherhood, make it seem like a love story from the beginning. There has to be a man, even if it's just the main character's husband. A lover would be good. As long as your focus is completely original. Have you read Amélie Nothomb? All that matters is the hook. Don't go into your own experience of motherhood—that won't interest anybody." That's what she said. Then she gutted a croissant with a serrated knife, popped a big bite in her canary head and looked out the window with a stuffed mouth.

I spent about six months thinking about how to be absolutely original.

They have a pistol to your head. You know you're going to die and you must say something. You can write. Think hard about what you will tell. And do it before the metal heats up because it's important that the weapon's coldness makes it onto the page. You can illuminate a single point of darkness on Earth. You can do it before everything blows up. So SPEAK. This is what it means to write against death. I used to write from the barrel of that gun. Or I tried to. The gunmetal was a turn on: I felt powerful writing just before death.

A three-year-old covers her eyes and starts to count. *One-four-two-seven.* She wants you to hide. Do it in the hedges, where she always looks first. When she finds you, she'll explode with laughter. She will laugh like there's no tomorrow or anything remotely like it, because there really is no tomorrow or anything like it. She will laugh with her arms open wide just before she hugs you. And she will look at the sky and say "CLOUD." And you will know that there is a part of life that exists beyond time. It isn't a point of darkness that you have to illuminate. It's a warm light that you just might be able to live in, for an instant. And once there, you will surely have nothing left to say. Where you are going, there are no words. So KEEP QUIET. This is what it means to write against life. So I will write this book. Maybe that's why I feel so fragile, just before starting to live.

TWO

I Can't Have Children

Let's get something straight: you can be a mother without having children. I was a mother long before I had D1 (five years old) and D2 (two and a half). And I'm not talking about the kids of the divorced guy I dated for three years. I'm talking about being a mother without children. Not your own, not someone else's. Unfortunately, for a long time I thought I couldn't learn about motherhood if I wasn't able to give birth. Poor thing. I thought I knew it all, but I didn't have a clue.

No one thinks of the father as simply "the one who inseminates." He isn't just sperm, racing to the finish line. The father figure isn't a physiological one. A father is … how can I put this? The one who creates. In the New Testament, there is a father and there is a virgin. There isn't much else to add.

The fact that I can't have children *naturally* is one of the reasons I've decided to write about motherhood. I believe my inability to conceive legitimizes my view on this subject: you've got to be a real woman to be barren.

I used to imagine the fertile woman as a moist, verdant mountain. I was wrong, sure, but it wasn't all in my head. The image has been etched in stone and time, rounded out like the womb of a Paleolithic Venus by our market-driven culture. But embryos can't implant in love or TV ads brimming with families and diapers. Expectation isn't fertile soil for life. Expectation is always barren. I know now that what my daughters needed was a wound in which to nest, the fallow earth I carried inside.

Sooner or later, we all become sterile. It doesn't matter whether a woman has given birth to four, five, or twelve babies—we're all doomed to the same end. Make no mistake: a child is a means of desiccation. One fine day, a child will look her mother in the eye and make it clear she'll never be fertile again.

I've been infertile for as long as I can remember. Even as a girl, the proof had been in my underwear, always a pristine white. An unpolluted message: if you don't bleed, you don't bear. I suppose, in that sense, I felt like a man. The thing they say about the lucky guy. A fortunate woman. I loved not bleeding. I felt a bit like "the chosen one" when at fourteen, fifteen, sixteen, seventeen, I didn't have to plug up a monthly hemorrhage. I pitied my friends.

At university, blood acquired another meaning. I started hearing about female poets and their red words and thoughts made flesh. The words were even redder when the poets were French. They all said *placenta, period, uterus, vagina, menstruation, ovaries, vulva, belly, pubis, guts, blood* (female poets are bloody and fierce), *womb, breasts, hormones, eggs* ... at this rate, I thought, our work will never make it off the tampon shelf.

I was sure writing didn't have to be a kind of hemorrhage but, instead, could be a kind of culture. I didn't want to bleed under any circumstances. I was going to write a thesis, go to work, be successful. I wanted men to read me too, and I didn't plan to write the word *uterus* for anything in the world. I was practically a guy, after all.

But time passed. As the other girls became something else, I was still sterile and starting to get old. The year I did my first round of in vitro, the extraordinarily young poet Luna Miguel published an anthology titled *Sangrantes*

(Bleeders), a book of twenty-nine women giving blood a poetic form. The girls from university had started down their own kind of paths, serpentine and narrow, while I was standing clueless and alone in the middle of a wide highway.

Women trying to get pregnant are unhappy when their periods come, but I never even really got mine. I caught a whiff of blood two or three times a year if I was lucky, sometimes not at all. I didn't feel ashamed or anything, but it was an absence, knocking on all my doors, squeezing in between the bars on my windows. Every day.

Knock knock.

It's me! The Idea. Can I come in?

No.

Okay, I'll just wait for you downstairs in the new bodega, over by the oranges.

Knock knock.

I'm on your steering wheel and your laptop keyboard, I'm always with you.

Knock knock.

I lie on your pillow at night. You can hear me breathing. Won't you let me in? I come in the name of the cosmos.

Two blue checks in WhatsApp. Message received.

The universe says you shouldn't be here, that nobody wants girls of your lineage. You were nearsighted, you had astigmatism, you have that problem with your wisdom teeth, and your hair is too straight. That tear in your meniscus was no accident—you have been judged. It's all over. Woman, you are sterile. Woman, you don't bleed. Woman, you aren't a woman. Woman, you are nothing. Woman, disappear.

Being infertile wasn't good.

I have MyMother's compassionate face before me: there is so much love for me inside MyMother. I have Man before me, too: he says he doesn't want to raise a child that's been born already. He wants our love to bear a child. I think that, potentially, our love isn't as perfect as he might believe, that there's a deep well in it, that we are a litany of shadows and bad luck. But I don't tell him that. I keep my thoughts about us and everything that's wrong to myself.

The Idea of not being a mother, of never being a mother, hit me like a bolt of lightning to the skull. It wasn't a set-back, or disappointment; it was something else, something that split my life in two. Losing the child that will never come goes way beyond sorrow. After all, sorrow can live alongside joy. Sorrow can even be the ballast that keeps us afloat, sometimes. I have no problem with sorrow. But the Idea of never being a mother is something else, it takes on so many shapes that it can invade you completely. Inside a woman's body, the Idea of never being a mother is a cancer.

Before me now, I have the fertility clinic gynecologist's shiny hair, smoothed by a straightener. One by one, she goes over every item on the bill we're about to pay. Ovarian stimulation: 500 euros. Oocyte extraction: 1,200 euros. IVF lab: 1,500 euros. Transfer of embryos: 300 euros. Then she points to another part of the page. *Possible extras*, I read in bold as the doctor silently points to the items we won't be charged for yet, the extras still to come. Micro-injection of sperm: 650 euros. Freezing of embryos: 800 euros. Hatching: 400 euros. Anesthesia: 300 euros. Transfer of frozen embryos: 850 euros. Cultivation of embryos in an EmbryoScope incubator: 350 euros.

When the Idea shows up, it creates a hollow. The hollow is how we women define what we lack. Not lack as in needing milk in the fridge, a car in the garage, or even weekly deposits in an emotional bank account. My hollow was all of the terror that T. S. Eliot attributed to a handful of dust when he wrote *The Waste Land*. And it was that dust on my kitchen floor. It was MyMother, my aunts, and my grandmother sweeping that dust. Over centuries. Millennia of women grasping their brooms. It was me, crouching down, dragging all the dust toward the dustpan, depositing it into the trashcan every night, all the nights. There is so much dust in a home.

Every woman I know has this hollow, this hole. You're a woman and they tell you "The hollow is coming" and you're scared stiff. A man says to a woman: "I can fill that hole." And she falls in love or gets married or something like it. He could be an angel or a puppet, as Rilke would say. But she'll still feel the hole. Being born with the hollow: that's being a woman. And that's being a mother.

I leave the pharmacy with the receipt for everything I'm going to take in my attempt to become one of those women with designated parking spaces at the grocery store and reserved metro seats. With swollen breasts and bellies and that way of moving and speaking. Powerful and arbitrary, young goddesses capable of containing something other than emptiness.

Puregon follicle stimulating hormone (FSH), 900 IU	359.00 euros
Puregon, 600 IU	274.74 euros
Cetrotide injections, 7.25 mg vials	248.70 euros
Ovitrelle injections, 250 mg, 1 dose	50.63 euros
Blastoestimulina vaginal treatment, 10 ovules	6.95 euros
Zithromax, 1 gm, 1 packet	3.93 euros
Azithromycine, 500 mg, 3-day pack	5.90 euros
Progeffik progesterone, 250 mg, 60 pills	38.90 euros
Total:	988.75 euros

There is nothing filthy about paying to be a mother, but still I slip my receipt into my wallet with the same smooth movement as a client sliding bills over a hooker's naked breast. Something isn't right in those numbers, an injustice that makes me feel guilty.

Long before they were born, I sensed the abyss my daughters would eventually open inside of me, and I thought that words were the only way to make meaning, to seal up that bottomless shaft, the terror. And so I wrote. But the words were never mine. Someone else said *pencil* and *kiss* and *flour* and *rat* long before I ever did, thousands of years before. So long before that the words arrived stale to my lips. Obviously, you can't fill the hole with something that isn't yours.

When I found out I couldn't have children, the words I knew went blank, white like my underwear. Useless. So I started to gather up all the lies I had believed. Because words are lies, too:

Our bodies, our choice; Just Do It; I think therefore I am; When you're a mother, you'll understand; I'm going to leave my wife; Podemos; I'm your friend; There is a political ETA and an armed ETA; I've been tested and I don't have AIDS; May the Force be with you; Who cares what I say …

These were things I was told. And I believed them all. Becoming a mother, by contrast, would be a kind of truth. It had to be.

Four years ago: D1 is in her clear plastic bassinet beside my bed. I've just arrived from the recovery room after my C-section. My abdomen and uterus are scraped and freshly stitched. Every time I look at her, it hurts: an electric pinch in my belly and milk straining and stretching my pendulous breasts. Eternity wounds us with the force of an instant.

Man lays her on my lap and she curls like a promise.

Right now I know that as long as D1 breathes, my abyss will remain sealed. She is the key to that other world, the world where one lives without fissures. And she is truth.

A mother's womb is a place in the world. And the time comes when a woman knows it. And she's often prepared to do whatever it takes to cradle that bit of life, the site where the world finally makes sense. I was prepared to do whatever it took. And that place was truth. And it was a lie.

A creature nests in the hollow of motherhood: it is the offspring of a serpent. And the snake has been our enemy from the days of the first garden. "Because you have done this, cursed are you among all animals and among all wild creatures," God said. "Upon your belly you shall go and dust you shall eat all the days of your life. I will put enmity between you and the woman, and between your offspring and hers; he will strike your head, and you will strike his heel."

When you get pregnant, everyone makes the exact same claim: *Words cannot explain what you are about to feel and discover. You will understand everything once you are a mother.* But what can't be put into words is still said without them. Those wordless lies coil inside us like silent snakes. And motherhood is a knife without a handle: impossible to wield without getting cut.

THREE

On Horseback or In Diapers

Imagine a man between twenty-five and forty years old walking into a store for fathers. His first child is due in just a few days. You can imagine your own father (if you had one, that is), your boyfriend, the father of your children, an actor. If it happens to be winter, I'd prefer that he wear a trench coat. If it's summer, I don't want him in sandals (this is my story, after all).

"I'm here to buy my first superhero cape," the man says. "How much?"

"Well, that depends," the clerk replies. "Do you need it for flying between skyscrapers, leaving Earth's orbit, or high-angle space shots?"

Okay, now imagine another man and another store. This time, choose whomever you want as the father-to-be. He's going to buy a horse and a revolver, or maybe a shotgun (he hasn't decided yet). We're talking about a real man here, so he already has a hat. He could be wearing a baseball cap, beret, hood, wool hat, or straw boater, but his head is covered, that's for sure. Probably with a cowboy hat.

"How many bullets do you need?" the shopkeeper asks. "You need to know how many enemies you'll be facing, sir."

"Hard to say," the man replies. "But I'll need to protect my wife and children."

"In that case, we can't skimp on the ammunition."

"I agree."

"What do you do for a living?"

"I'm in construction," says the man. *I'm a writer. I'm a waiter. I'm a doctor. I'm all men.*

Now, imagine this is for real. That all the boys who ever played cowboys and Indians or cops and robbers were given arrows and guns, wives and children, and told to grow up and become men once and for all. My question is whether shooting a million imaginary bullets bears any relation at all to actually firing a gun.

I'm thirty-six years old when I go to the nearest pharmacy for the first pack of diapers I'll ever buy in my life.

"I think it's time to buy diapers," I say, gesturing toward my belly. I've gained forty-six pounds.

"How far along are you?"

"Thirty-eight weeks."

"In that case, the baby will be full term, so I won't show you anything for preemies. For newborns, diapers start at five pounds and then eight pounds. Do you know what your baby weighs?"

"Six pounds, according to the latest ultrasound."

"In that case, we'll start from eight pounds up. You're going to have a beautiful baby. These come in packs of fifty," the pharmacist says.

The diapers are beautiful. They're exactly like the ones I used to put on Nenuco Feliz, my childhood doll, my first baby, that piece of plastic. When I turned its head, its eyes rolled from side to side. I never got rid of it. I still have it somewhere, the head in one plastic bag and the body in another.

"I'm also going to need pacifiers, a thermometer, fingernail scissors, and bottles."

"Any brand in particular?"

"I want the kind that came with my Famosa dolls. I'd

like to find one of those pouches with the baby's name embroidered in pink, like the ones that came with Bath-time Nenuco. And, if possible, I want a clear plastic toiletry kit with fuchsia backstitching like my Barbie-with-Twins had. She always brought it to the park. She was a very organized doll."

"You'll find all the accessories you need in our display case. Do you plan to use latex or silicone nipples? Latex are softer, but some say that the silicone won't shape the baby's palate. And then there's the option of not using a pacifier, of course."

"I'll take one of everything. And a thermometer and bottle."

"Are you going to breastfeed?"

"Of course. But you don't practice that with dolls. I don't know if I'll be able to."

"That'll be forty-two euros."

I have a Law degree, two Masters—one in Marketing and the other in Creative Writing—I'm an executive creative director in one of the biggest agencies in Madrid. In other words, I'm a young professional with a solid career. Although I'm not so young anymore, to be honest. I've gotten old. I suppose this is why I'm out buying diapers. Now the question is: is playing mama to my dollies at all the same as raising a real baby? The sad answer is that, at this moment, I'd swear that it is.

Almost everything I know about motherhood I learned from playing with my dolls, whose legs I pulled off or whose faces I colored with marker. And it was fine. I'm an only child. I never saw my mother nurse or take care of anyone other than me, not that I think I have anything to learn from my mother and her friends. Because I'm the first of my line. I'll give my daughters bows and arrows and baby dolls and bottles and Batman capes and colored pencils and far fewer pink things than I had. The age-old figure of the mother raising her kids without leaving the house is dying, dying alone after having given so much, isolated by the walls of a home that encompassed MyMother's female universe. Walls that protected that precarious and prescribed space, separate from the rules of men and connected to her friends by the green phone in the kitchen. MyFather died when I was four and yet MyMother-the-widow still lived by men's rules, the same as all her married friends, the same as all women. She thought that doing the "normal thing" would be a way to protect us, the two of us. But the walls that protected also imprisoned and I want to knock them all down. I plan to build my own house—I'm sure of that.

There's a door behind the counter at this pharmacy, where I've come for my first flesh-and-blood baby's diapers. A big old wooden door. I haven't seen a door that size since I read the Kafka story "Before the Law."

Before the law stands a door-keeper. A man from the country comes to this door-keeper and asks for entry into the law. But the door-keeper says he cannot grant him entry now. The man considers and then asks if that means he will be allowed to enter later. "It is possible," says the door-keeper, "but not now." Since the door to the law stands open, as it always does, and the door-keeper steps to one side, the man bends to look through the door at the interior.

Kafka never describes the door to the Law, but it's obviously the same one as I have before me. And the pharmacist is, naturally, my door-keeper. The door is slightly ajar, but I can't see what is behind it. The counter keeps me from peering in.

Kafka's man from the country spends his whole life in front of that door, waiting for his moment, until the very day of his death. Then, with his final breath, he asks the door-keeper why, if everyone seeks the Law, he's the only one who has asked to enter for so many years. And the door-keeper roars in his ear: "Nobody else could gain admittance here, this entrance was meant only for you. I shall now go and close it." End of story.

The door scares me. I'm not sure I want to enter, but this is obviously my door and I know this because I've read more than that man from the country. I won't wait for my death to open it, even though I'm not ready to walk through. I'm afraid it will lead to my old bedroom where I used to rock my first doll and I'll see myself as an old woman, clutching the same toy.

I've been preparing to buy actual diapers my whole life. And now that it's finally happening, I'm not up to the task. I mothered all of my dolls up until I was eight or nine, when my other dolls, the ones with breasts (Barbie, Nancy, Chabel ...) became mothers to their own children. Where are my old friends now?

"Forty-two euros," the woman repeats on the other side of the counter.

"Yes, sorry," I reply.

I firmly punch my PIN on the keypad offered by the aged hand of the female pharmacist. My PIN opens the door to money. I look at the enormous slab of wood behind the woman and am certain I also know its password.

That very night, stealthily and in pajamas, I make my way back to the door behind the counter. I know I have to go in. I know it's there for me, waiting.

Barefoot, I walk Madrid's old cobblestones toward the glass-doored pharmacy on the corner. My bottoms drag on the ground because I'm wearing Primark pajamas made for a giantess. Size XXL: perfect for a woman much, much taller than me but with a waist like mine—157 lbs in 66 inches. I'm wearing the pajamas of a giantess and it's possible I'll meet with one when I cross the threshold. What if she's a gigantic midwife? Or even a pink-horned unicorn?

Anyone in there? I knock on the pharmacy door, which opens soundlessly. The pharmacist must be in bed. It's very dark. Nothing and no one inside, just the darkness, pitch black until my eyes adjust and I sense a shadowy light and begin to make out the shape of the room and the figures inside. At first, they're so still that they look like mannequins, but I soon detect the first movements. I finally see them. They are women. There are lots of them chatting in little groups. I can't quite see to the back of the room; it could be a garage, or a weapons hall in a castle. But it's immense and diaphanous. The village Agora with cement floors. Like me, all the women are barefoot.

One of them—big, tall, and blond, the strongest and most fragile among them (her eyes as transparent and bright as a bolt of lightning)—approaches and takes both of my hands in hers.

"We've been waiting for you," she whispers in my ear. "Welcome."

"I shouldn't be here," I say, making excuses the stranger doesn't deserve. "I want to leave right this instant."

"Then go," she replies. "But I must tell you something before you do."

"Hurry," I say.

"When the baby is born, don't knock down all the walls. Let at least one stand. Remember that the wind can be a terrible bother, even on the best beaches. And arrange to have an older mother with you. She will know more than you from having made mistakes, regardless of all the times you plan to be right."

"Will I ever see you again?"

"I don't think so. This entrance was destined for you alone. And now that you've come, I will close it."

FOUR

On Failure and Bubble Gum

I don't watch the sky. I never watch the sky. And I don't know if a child will happen for me. I think about death every day. And I love sex. It fills me with another life, refills me. Fills the hollow. Sex grounds me—but it won't create a place for my children.

The doctors, by nature, won't make any guarantees. My doctor has her black locks in a French braid, not a single piece out of place. Hair as tight as a bowstring. Her words are arrows. "It depends a great deal on the woman's age and the attendant factors contributing to the diagnosis. Generally speaking, the average rate of pregnancy per cycle is somewhere between 45% and 50%, although deviations result from each individual case. The average rate of pregnancy after three cycles is 75%. The risk of miscarriage is about 15% per cycle. When transferring frozen-thawed embryos, the average rate of success is about 25% per attempt, compared to 35% for embryos that underwent flash vitrification." I calculate the probability of saving the 30,000 euros it will cost me to achieve the unlikely 80% chance of becoming a mother.

Doctors won't make guarantees. My doctor has years of schooling behind her but she isn't going to answer any of my questions. It doesn't matter if the treatments last months or years. Good doctors never talk about what they don't know, because they believe in science. Good writers *only* talk about what they don't know, because they believe in magic. Though it's also true that there is no science without poetry. This doctor and I should understand one another.

She keeps reciting her magic numbers, like she's casting a spell. When she's done, she says, "You'll have to sign a consent form that stipulates what to do in the event that the father dies during the course of treatment. The law allows for the transfer of embryos up to twelve months after the father's death in the case of the couple's prior consent. The paperwork is pretty tedious, but it's required to proceed." I'm beginning to think that a woman like her can't help a woman like me.

"In the event of his death during the course of treatment, Mr. _____ , of legal age, with National ID number _____ consents to the use of his genetic material (in the event of its cryopreservation in this center) during the twelve months following his demise in order to impregnate Ms./Mrs. _____ and secure the legal registration of both parents on the birth record (circle the chosen option)."

He circles *yes* before he even adds his name. The doctor goes to get the credit card machine so we can swipe and make the payment. As she walks away, I make a joke about that Quevedo poem on love outlasting death. Man winks. He's winked at me many times before, always when no one is looking, always when we're in some kind of trouble.

Next, we sign all the forms, side by side in our chairs.

There are three types of women who hang around fertility clinics and speak to female destiny, apart from the doctor, of course: actresses, princesses, and football players' wives and girlfriends. They are always there, in the waiting rooms. Those women and their full-color, glossy pronouncements on motherhood, so thin and just out of labor every time they open their mouths. Women who are always the face of some brand, women who obscure the images of other women who aren't conceived in the market. The rest of us, in other words: the infertile, the old, the lesbians, hypnotically leafing through the pages of celebrity, fashion, and beauty magazines. The kinds of magazines women supposedly read. The thesis, according to the experience of these female protagonists, is always the same: having a baby is the external confirmation that you deserve to live. There are nuances, beyond that initial fact. For example, Penélope Cruz: "Having children is like throwing yourself off a cliff, it changes your life forever, but it also teaches you to fly. Motherhood is the most enjoyable experience in the world."

The worst thing that can happen to you in the waiting room of a fertility clinic is to insert a tampon and then feel it inside you as you read something like this. "Becoming a mother has changed me. It's one of the most powerful experiences in my life," continues Penélope, who has quit weaving her shroud and no longer waits. I can also confirm that for some artists, children naturally enhance their talents. As with Shakira: "Motherhood has even changed my voice."

Private fertility clinics are full of celebrity magazines because they serve as the best marketing tool for the business. Actresses talk about family vacations, about their next projects. Football wives show off their babies' walk-in closets, because there are babies who have walk-in closets. They all repeat that they're happy, that everything is turning out well, that they never imagined they could be so complete, that the chosen father is undoubtedly the most wonderful man on earth, a mirror image, naturally, of the most wonderful woman.

In these magazines, there is a scene that illustrates

motherhood as powerfully as the Nativity story represents the family. The woman, dressed in house clothes (preferably a nightgown), lies on a couch or bed and gazes at her baby or her belly. And the man, in street clothes (preferably a suit), gazes at them both from the opposite corner of the room. He has either just come home or is about to leave the house. She is the house. And the baby is a new room. Then they take a photo all together. They look at the camera and they smile at the *click*. They say everything will turn out fine, even if something isn't going right, even if the baby is sick, even if they miscarry. All that matters is that those women want to *have*. And so they do. And this makes me want to laugh. Can you imagine *having* being enough? They show off tattoos of their offspring's names on intimate parts of their bodies for all the world to see: the forearm and the inside of the wrist are the preferred locations. And they all tell the same story: motherhood is a miracle that can make any woman a better woman. That is the motherhood myth. The big con.

The idea that women self-realize as individuals through motherhood is a universal value in all cultures: to be a mother is the chance for any female (because all females can do it, even mediocre and graceless ones, all females, that is, except infertile ones) to reach the moon without leaving the house, a chance to attain intimate, interior fulfillment, to explore the universe by cupping her belly. In the clinic's waiting room, thirty or forty thousand euros doesn't seem like a lot of money. Because being a mother will give me superpowers, it will fatten me up and impregnate me with wisdom and courage and truth. And, most importantly, it will be *an unforgettable experience*.

Sometimes I think we've made motherhood complicit

with mediocrity. Who hasn't heard one woman say to another, "You'll understand when you're a mother"? The woman who utters this sentence is always the dumber of the two. And there's something even worse. One woman saying to another woman—older, brilliant, independent, childless—"If you were a mother, you'd understand."

Keep chomping on your failure as if it were a huge wad of bubble gum. It will fill your mouth, leaving no room for the slightest bit of hope to stick between your teeth. Nothing.

After you've been plugged with a pair of embryos, you can't fuck for a while. They say it's for safety reasons, but I think it's so there's no doubt that you owe your children to Science. No fucking for fifteen days. We won't make love for the four weeks that we wait. I would give up anything—eating, moving, peeing—just to keep that embryo from escaping me. But it won't make a difference. My space won't fill. It's empty, despite our abstinence.

Looking back, I don't know how I managed to get through it. I'm not talking about the infertility or the shots or the hormones or the tests or the now-wait-again, the clinical hiccups. I'm referring solely to the celebrity magazines in the waiting room. The option of locking myself in the clinic's shiny bathroom with a pack of Gillette razors and ending it all in there seemed plausible. Either that or cleaning the place spotless, go figure. Give the bathroom—where all the infertile women before me have peed—a good scrubbing, find a way to collect the rose-colored urine of the mothers-to-be, the alchemic power of life that converts the blank stripe on a pregnancy test into a baby-pink affirmation. I only ever used the Clearblue e-tests. They communicate with the user via words on a digital screen. You read: *Not pregnant*. The instruction pamphlet is misleading: the lack of the fucking second pink line means more than just "not pregnant." The absence of a double line is pure alchemy and what it really says is: "You are not magic. Your urine smells like piss. Give up."

I was lucky. I found Jen in the waiting room. Jennifer Aniston saved my life: "Having a baby isn't the measure of my happiness or success in life, my achievements, or anything else," and "Motherhood doesn't determine a woman's worth." We live in a world in which words like Jen's rarely make headlines; they represent the start of a debate and not a universal truth like Shakira's new voice. Say it again, Jen: "Motherhood doesn't determine a woman's worth." And although she isn't a mother, she and I have reached the same conclusion by different means: "Motherhood doesn't determine a woman's worth." Two daughters later, I'll just add a little something to that statement: "Motherhood doesn't determine the worth of a woman *who has never been a mother.*" But what about the rest of us? Good grades measure a student's worth; good sex, a lover's. A good job title is how we determine a professional's value, a good goal for an athlete, a good book for a writer ... What determines a woman's worth after she becomes a mother? And to whom should she be compared: to a man, to a woman without children? How many hours a day does a mother have to go on living as if she were just a woman, without thinking about, tending to, or responding to her child? And what if she also earns a salary to feed that child and takes her to school and comforts her in the middle of the night and nourishes her with milk from her body?

Explaining her mindset before writing *The Second Sex*, Simone de Beauvoir recounts that she never felt inferior for being a woman, that femininity had never been a burden for her. Being a woman has never hindered her, she recalled telling Sartre. That's how Simone used to think before she started to seriously consider her condition as a woman. Sure, there are lots of women for whom being *a woman* isn't a burden, even after someone has explained to them all the invisible weight we carry, not to mention the weight shouldered by all the women who are invisible. But I've never met and I've never read any woman for whom motherhood wasn't a weight, either before or after. It's been so obvious for so long, it didn't even seem worth writing about.

So there's the burden and there's the music. All of it real and all of it simultaneous. It doesn't matter what, or where, we read about motherhood. It doesn't matter if it's an elated actress or a mother with regrets; an underlying text always exists. The music of life can be perceived even in the celebrity magazines and, sometimes, the murmur of lyrics to a melody.

Trying for a baby, I wrote in the notebook I carried around back then and am reading again now. This isn't a quote from some famous woman. I've heard MyMother saying the same thing to a friend: "My daughter is trying." It's everywhere, pay attention and you'll notice that we only reproduce because at some point we *try*: we're trying for a baby, they're going to go for it, he's always wanted to try for a third, let's do it, let's try. What is it everyone is trying? How will they accomplish their babies? At a better clinic than mine?

Before I'm inseminated with fertilized, vitrified embryos, I'm shown them on a screen. They are brilliant blue and float, dragonflies skimming over water. They are incredibly alive but they won't stay with me, despite their exceptional genetic quality. Group A, the geneticist happily pronounces. The best embryos will have to fail first, before the doctor introduces a silver syringe with microscopic embryos of worse quality, the thawed ones we are required to use before starting another cycle. Everybody knows that in the freeze-thaw process, a little something is lost. But I'm not trying for a perfect lab baby. Nor am I interested in expectations or assurances, I don't need those where I'm going. Not anymore. To have a child means both accepting the futility of *trying*, the impotence of our mortal insistence, and having faith in the breath of eternity, the sigh of life that animates us, opens our eyes.

Our attempts—mortal, definitive—and not conception, are what make mothers of us, women and men alike. You lift your eyes beyond Earth's heavy mantle and feel that something is right. And trust. And wait.

I know now. In the gynecologist's chair where I open my legs to receive you, your father's hand on the arm of a green chair in the opposite corner, far from me, I know. I try, and I am a mother. Whether or not you will come, at this very moment, right now: I am your mother.

The chair with its stirrups is both throne and stallion. And from up here, my mind as cool as the steel under my thighs, I know: I am your mother and I will write about you.

Beatrice am I, who do bid thee go;
I come from there, where I would fain return;
Love moved me, which compelleth me to speak.

Dante, *The Divine Comedy*, canto II, verses 70–73

FIVE

The Desire

There's something perverse in wanting to have a child. Something murky. I know this, I've known it from the beginning. But there I was: my uterus pulsing like a satisfied sex, from the bar at the pub straight into the gynecologist's exam chair.

Make no mistake. Motherhood is as empty a desire as love can be. Who hasn't said "I love you" just to change the subject? Love can be a refuge from the elements and despair. Or it can be love.

You say "I want to be a mother" and everyone bows down before your courage, you are queen. Your family, boss, and friends lower their heads and act as if, for once, life had some sort of meaning. But not MyMother. She says, "I just can't understand how you can want something like that. You don't *want* children, you have them and that's it. I wouldn't have had you, if I had thought it through. I don't regret it. But from the day you were born until I die, I'll be your mother."

Most women are like MyMother. Women who had babies or will have them, period. Life will bestow babies upon them, regardless of what they do. Like when my friend Liliana told me about her distinct lack of maternal ambition and got pregnant within days. So what? To be born, children need a woman's body, not her desire. Except in defective cases like mine.

A woman is crying inconsolably in a kitchen with a greasy stovetop and a pile of dishes in the sink. There's a ball she can't attend and a prince she won't meet. A fairy appears and gives her a pair of glass slippers and a sky-blue dress. The fairy turns a pumpkin into a carriage and sends the woman off to triumph at the party.

A man is asleep. He isn't weeping or wailing, he's at rest. He lays his head on a stone for a pillow. Now he dreams. He sees a glorious staircase uniting Heaven and Earth, used by the angels. Suddenly, God is at his side. Instead of a carriage, He's come to bestow the man with a path. He says, "The land on which you lie I will give to you and to your offspring; and your offspring shall be like the dust of the earth, and you shall spread abroad to the west and to the east and to the north and to the south; and all the families of the earth shall be blessed in you and in your offspring."

God is a man speaking to another man. There are no angels or stairways for women who want—only disappointment and glass slippers.

I want.

To have.

A child.

Six words. I want + to have. How much does the verb *to have* diminish the worthiest of desires?

I want love, I want that purse, I want a healthy body, I want to marry you, I want this book to be published, I want a house. And now: I want to have love, I want to have that purse, I want to have a healthy body, I want to have you married to me, I want to have a house. Possession is a trap, it always has been.

To have + a child. Isn't this even worse?

It starts with wanting to have a child and ends with a claim for child tax credit. There's a box to check for the mortgage, one for salary, another for children. Words are a trap: we are certain that what can be *had* can be *bought*.

I want + a child = Problem. Because a wish fulfilled is over and done with.

Obtain your heart's desire—or two or three of them—just like you've happened upon the genie in the lamp. Then add ten years and see what happens. Dreams have stretch, they give a bit, like panties. My favorite pair, for example, were chiffon with red and green flowers. My go-to on many mornings, until one day I put them on and they didn't fit my skin, it was like they belonged to another woman. I had to throw them out. Impossible, when this happens, to know whether it's the body or the article of clothing that has changed first. With the passage of time, neither one is what it once was.

And will not time come to rest upon my daughters as well? I thought it wouldn't. I was sure it wouldn't. And before I had them, I repeated it to myself on many nights: "I want to have a child." I whispered it to Man, too, and he would stroke my hair before we fell asleep.

I want + to have + a child = Wrong.

If it were just a question of having, adoption would be a fine option. If you want to have a dog, for example, everybody knows your best bet is to adopt one. Regardless of whether it's just a pup or advanced in years, adopted dogs are obviously the nobler choice. And their owners feel superior to the people who buy an animal in a store: every breed has a price, despite the fact that we all know it's wrong to pay for these kinds of things.

I didn't want to adopt, even though I knew that paying to have a baby with my own genetic material wasn't right. It was much worse than buying a Dalmatian from a puppy mill. Undoubtedly, adoption was the morally superior option. But I wanted a *purebred* baby.

Luckily, there is a social understanding with respect to what an infertile woman—or a single woman, or a single man, or two men—or whoever *wants* (+) *to have* (+) *a baby* must do in order to become a mother: spend every cent she has, as well as open a few lines of credit, before adopting a child. We live deeply ingrained in an ideology of difference, one in which we consider ourselves so unique that we want to grant our children the same distinction. But ideology is a veil that conceals another reality: our DNA is 99.9% the same as the DNA of any other human being. The difference between us (regardless of race or sex) is genetically and objectively irrelevant. Nevertheless, thanks to a narcissistic ideology of uniqueness, no one questions the ethics of paying to become a mother (or father) without attempting to adopt an already-living child who *needs* one.

The same people who adopt their darling pets and are publically opposed to the sale of purebred puppies can go on in detail about how a newborn human baby (not to mention the ones who are already a year or two old) can never be entirely trusted. This might not be logical, but it is human: children are not dogs. This is all said in fertility clinics and on internet forums, of course. Adopting a baby is like Russian roulette: the child could be sick, or ugly, or disobedient; it could be stupid or a different color or develop intolerable behaviors. Who wants a child like that? Fortunately, as everyone knows, biological children are predictable and always turn out well.

Evidently, someone who *really wants to have a baby* has no interest in adopting one. Because the difference between an adopted child and a biological one is that the adopted child cannot be dreamed up. By contrast, you can dump all the desire and possession you want onto a biological child. An adopted child will never be yours entirely—not exclusively—because he or she subverts the idea of ownership. And for some people, people like me, this makes them worse as children. An adopted child would have demanded an understanding of love and of the world that I do not possess.

So like a monster, I grew fat with maternal desire, with all the power of my imagination and my ideology. Secretly, without telling a soul, I wanted my first child to be a girl. More concretely, a healthy girl. Intelligent. A girl who would have curls until she was two or three; after that, it would be better if her hair grew straight. A girl who would like reading more than math. Capable of looking after her friends and inhabiting the world with all the passion life deserves. It goes without saying that my imaginary daughter would be a happy child. Biological children always are. Happy, with dark-brown eyes. Who wouldn't want a child like that?

Luckily for my daughters, people aren't dogs. And human beings can, on occasion, overcome even their mothers.

SIX

And Mother Saw That It Was Good

The maternity ward in a hospital is a dimly lit space where flowers wilt in the hallway. Hospital windows don't open, and this strengthens the scent of the flowers wrapped in plastic sleeves, their stems choked by enormous bows. At night, the flowers are removed from the rooms because they're apparently bad for newborns. They suck up all the air (or so MyMother says). This must be what everyone thinks, because there is a kind of floral competition that occurs outside the rooms. *How strange, that room doesn't have any flowers: she must be dilating. Only two bouquets: she must have just had the baby.*

MyMother likes taking our flowers out to the hallway. They make her proud, in their pots and wicker baskets, or in tomato-sauce jars she scrounged up for the bouquets that arrive without a vase. The mother who receives the most flowers is clearly the most fortunate, as if the most celebrated baby will be more charming, more intelligent, happier than the others.

On my last day in the hospital, there are so many flowers that she has to pile them up in front of the door, a mound the likes of which I had only seen at funerals. I felt like the bad witch we hadn't invited to the delivery would show up at any moment: "It doesn't matter how many people love you, my dear, sooner or later someone will try to hurt you."

But the witch doesn't even need to appear. Those flowers, all those flowers, are the first curse. All those expectations. All those petals like plucked dreams falling on our faces, one after another, until we can't breathe. In a few days, those flowers will be dead.

Some women say that the birth of their first child was the happiest day of their life. Not so, in my case. Vertigo and light, sure. Like when I was little and watched fireworks explode over the sea, my hands over my ears, screaming as loud as I could, deaf to all but the burst of color. The kind of radiant, mortal scream you let out on a rollercoaster, a carnival attraction set up by men with holes in their jeans, and where your crush puts their arm around your waist for the first time.

I returned to those screams in the delivery room; I faced the gunpowder from my first firecracker, the first lie my first crush told me, all the other fear I held in my heart. They told me I needed a C-section. An epidural. And I needed to sit very straight, very still, waiting for the pinch that would put my body to sleep.

A pinch between your vertebrae and the world comes undone. It starts with the tip of the big toe on my left foot. Then the other. I can't feel my toes, I don't have feet. I can't feel my knees and I lose my biceps, my thighs are erased, even my vagina. But I can still hear and see perfectly. I can smell. But my body has disappeared and I am weightless. It's just my flesh that has been switched off. The soul remains intact, maybe even more awake: the interference fades, now that the body is silent. And so I wait for you, naked and open, literally open on the sterile steel of the operating table.

D1 arrived with her eyes glued shut and fists clenched and I heard her first cry, soft as a bird in my breast. And we spoke. "Welcome, D1. I'm your mother. That's all you have to know to be here. Because now you are."

SEVEN

To Sing a Lullaby

The first word, the very first word, was spoken by a woman. A soothing sound, almost a moan. Before my daughters, I had been mute in the midst of so much noise. The noise of words, resumés, books, electronic music.

I make this discovery the night I sing D1 a lullaby: it's not even a song, maybe nothing more than a rhythm, or a rite. My first words free of judgment and thought.

D1 has been crying all night: my nipples are red from bringing her to my breast. I've changed two dry diapers, Man has walked her shrieking wail up and down the hallway, I've massaged her with calendula oil, wrapped her in the soothing embrace of her favorite swaddle, placed pillows on either side of the crib so she won't be scared by the enormity of the world outside the womb. I've brought her to my bed, held her, talked to her, fed her again. But D1 cries. She's going to cry the whole night, and she and I both know it. Hope is futile; there's no cause or reason. Her crying is a fact, and, like all pain, I can't anticipate its arrival or plan for its departure. We go out to the living room so that at least one of us (Man) can sleep.

Under the window, the floor is very cold. We live in a fourth-floor apartment in the middle of Madrid and I can see other windows, other homes, other silences where there is no crying, no lights except for the golden flicker of the television at dawn, that other fire. There is only one wish, a sole reason to live right here and right now: sleep. There is only one fear: falling asleep on my feet, closing my eyes, letting her drop.

I start to count slowly, calmly, as if deaf to her piercing fury.

One, two, three, four ... twenty-five, twenty-six ... fifty-five, fifty-six, fifty-seven ... one hundred twenty-three, one hundred twenty-four ...

Counting is a kind of consolation. I count while admitting to myself that I don't know how to deal with D1. I am a mother incapable of calming her child. All I do is count, measure how long we'll hold out and which of us will give in first.

The neighbor across the street (second on the right) steps out onto her balcony in a red fleece robe, cigarette in hand. Her hair is pulled back, and she's wearing thick black glasses she never has on when I see her at the market. I love when she appears—my spirits are instantly buoyed. She comes out to smoke in her red mantle and I feel the same thrill as when the cuckoo would pop out of the Swiss clock in my childhood bedroom. We've never spoken, but the woman across the street is my bridge to easier times. I hope she smokes two.

Before she goes back in, my neighbor rubs her arms to shake off the cold and I look down at D1, who sighs and opens her two enormous owl eyes. I'm a useless mother, a mother that cannot manage to help her only child fall asleep. At this moment, D1 doesn't look happy or intelligent. She isn't the baby I imagined. She isn't even blonde. D1 is a stranger who won't stop crying.

One, one, friend to no one
Two, two, I'll sing to you
Three, three, we'll climb a tree

I'm not sure whether I'm making the song up or if

someone sang it to me one night as a child. I think it might be a combination. Parts I remember and others I invent, but each line emerges vainglorious.

Four, four, off to the store
Five, five, we'll take a drive
Six, six, pick up sticks
Seven, seven, watermelon
Eight, eight, we'll get home late

D1 looks at me with the inquisitive expression of a latecomer to a party and lets her eyelids close, falling like a blanket over the cold.

Nine, nine, I'm keeping time

For a moment, I think I can.

Ten, ten, sing it again

It's a fact. I'm doing it. I'm singing D1 a lullaby.

The days are white
The nights are black
Evening is blue
And morning lilac

The struggle is over. D1 is sleeping deeply in my arms. My little girl has fought tooth and nail against all logic and all the guides and manuals and solutions that I attempt to stuff her with whenever she cries. And she has won. I sing to celebrate her victory.

Row, row, row your boat
Gently down the stream
Merrily, merrily, merrily, merrily
Life is but a dream

It's four o'clock in the morning by the time I no longer consider putting her in bed or going to sleep myself. I want to stay here all night, all the nights. Now come the songs I know, lyrics sung in voice that is both unrecognizable and my own.

The Man Who Sold the World (as sung by Kurt Cobain),

Hold On, Hold On (Marianne Faithfull), *Compatir* (Carla Morrison), *Hallelujah* (Leonard Cohen), *The Greatest* (Cat Power). I'm going to sing all the songs, even the embarrassing ones. *Bamboleo* (Julio Iglesias), *La de la mochila azul* (Pedrito Fernández), *Under the Sea* (the Little Mermaid) ...

Until tonight, I have been alone, but suddenly I can feel it: my heart beating just there, under her head. And D1's racing pulse beside it. And in the apartment across the street, the neighbor's heart beats, lazily. Three hearts that mark the rhythm of the night we're crossing together.

D1 grips my finger with her sparrow hand and pulls me, slowly, out of my cage. She opens the balcony doors and together we leap into the night's black abyss. We can fly.

And we do fly. We soar really high, all the way to the top of a mountain, the earth shining in the distance below. And on that summit at the top of the world, I speak to my daughter.

D1, I am going to give you the only thing that no one can ever take away.

D1, someday living will be a wound and you will have to heal yourself with a song.

D1, another woman could feed you with her milk, but only your mother can give you this nourishment.

D1, you won't remember tonight, but it will always be yours.

There would be more lullabies to come, of course, much later. More lullabies, more nights.

Years would pass before I would hear Clara Janés sing her collection of poems *Kampa*. D2 had been born by then. It was night again, but this time I was the child.

a mor

a mor va

mora va

murmura va

murmuraba

murmuraba

I had read the poem before but I hadn't understood it. I hadn't even known there was something to understand then. But when she spoke them, Clara's words became magic, a spell that conjured a place of pure consolation when sung to you.

Clara Janés doesn't have a TV or cellphone. She isn't on Facebook (she is, however, in the Royal Spanish Academy, so there's that). She sings her poems with a voice like the finest thread of light, at times so taut it could break, and at others, blind, the world.

The night I met her in a writing workshop, she told our select group of aspiring writers with great sadness how her home was once broken into and a gold medal stolen, a medal that had meant a great deal to her, it being a gift from Václav Havel. The thieves left behind paintings, books, other works of art that were more valuable. But what Clara missed, all those years later, was the golden luster that has nothing to do with an object's worth. Gold can be a shooting star. Or it can be real gold.

We mothers seek that golden moment. We would pay for it, sometimes. Love for it, for the luminescence that lights the path to love, but which isn't love itself. It is a glimmer. We might be giving our lives for a shooting star. Or for a will-o'-the-wisp.

The night I met Clara, she and her transparent eyes traveled back in time to long-ago conversations. And I knew then, we mothers are not alone, there are other prospectors, all the gold seekers who came before us.

Luckily—and to her chagrin, I suppose—Clara *is* on YouTube and I can listen to her anytime I want.

EIGHT

When D1 Cries, Man Smiles

No man is as perfect as the man who cares for your children, as the man who cares for your firstborn. No man is as perfect as Man when he's cradling D1.

Man is thirty-nine years old and a professor of the History of Ideas at the Complutense University in Madrid. He lives outside the market, protected by his department, which is actually a savage jungle in which no one feels safe. His summer vacation is almost as long as my maternity leave, so when D1 was born, I never felt alone. Man speaks Greek and has dedicated the past two years of his life to research on Elizabethan thinkers (John Dee, Christopher Marlowe, Walter Raleigh, and the like). Man believes in what he does and he is the sole master of his work. In this sense, he's a rare specimen.

One would assume that the world is still the same whether a man goes out in search of a white whale every morning, or whether, one day, that same man decides not to. But that isn't true. Perhaps Man won't find what he's looking for, but he's certainly not going to stop believing in it. In contrast, my work is at the service of whoever pays for it. We make a good team. He brings home the whales and I bring home the bacon.

The bad thing about the people who go looking for whales is that sometimes they succumb to discouragement. Paradoxically, this doesn't usually happen to those of us who work for money. We detest traffic jams and all of that, but we don't have time for moral exhaustion.

And I don't even earn that much.

Before D1, Man would forget some mornings why he had to go in to the university. He would get sad, stay home, loaf about.

"Being a researcher is impossible in this country," he'd say. For example.

"Don't forget to buy yogurt," I would reply.

These episodes aside, Man and I were happy before D1. Then she came, and with her, Man became the Father-OfMyFirstChild. There's a difference between Man and *that man.*

When D1 cries, the FatherOfMyFirstChild smiles.

Man is never upset by D1's wailing. With each cry comes another chance to tend to her, a gap in time when everything else can wait.

D1 is six months old and Man is standing in the corner of our bedroom, lifting her in his arms. They are both flesh, both naked, and both mine. We are hunters, we are gatherers, and we are all we need to stay warm.

That's how it was when D1 arrived. Love went off like a shot, flooded everything, as simple as that. During D1's first year, I became a pump, an inexhaustible fountain of love. I was sure I would have more children. I had love for more people than could fit in our house. I was literally overflowing. And, in large part, Man was to blame.

Something about Man holding D1 drew me irreversibly toward him. And sometimes, when we were alone with newborn D1, I felt a force propelling us beyond ourselves, outside of myself. It was love, urgent as a monsoon on the verge of leveling everything in its path.

I do know one thing: if it doesn't knock you flat, it isn't love.

The sky darkened, my vision grew cloudy and the clouds burst over the city, and in the midst of chaos—

just as the first buildings were sent flying through the air—we were brutally happy. As if in the middle of that storm everything made sense and we could now die in peace. Sometimes I think Man is the only person I won't grow tired of fucking. And that is, without a doubt, the reason why Man became the FatherOfMyFirstChild.

Long before that, I chased other men in hopes of conquering another type of meaning, another type of progenitor, another passion. Like my fling with Guy de Maupassant, father of the contemporary short story and favorite student of Gustave Flaubert.

"Boule de Suif"—translated variously as "Butterball," "Ball of Fat," "Dumpling"—was the first Maupassant story I ever read. I loved it. So subtle, so wounding.

Maupassant understood the meaning of life for a woman. Specifically, that we are born with two major roles, both of them delicious: motherhood and love.

Ball of Fat, the story's protagonist, is a prostitute in occupied France during the Franco-Prussian war who demonstrates how those of an apparently lower social class are superior in moral terms. And the lowest of the low is a woman, Maupassant my friend. The root lies deep underground.

In addition to his writings, Maupassant produced three children whom he never recognized in life: Honoré-Lucien, Jeanne-Lucienne, and Marguerite. He was a promiscuous man and a committed misogynist but, oddly, he only reproduced with one woman. We know almost nothing about her except her name, Joséphine Litzelmann, and her profession: seamstress. Maupassant's biographers refer to her as "the lady in gray" because of her appearance in photographs.

I was born almost a century after the man who inspired me to write my first story. I'm thirty-six, D1 is just six months old, and thanks to Flaubert's disciple I know there are only three important things for me to do: make love, give birth, and die. The same for my daughters, according to Maupassant. I also know that we women are but a gray smudge, like the seamstress Joséphine Litzel-mann, and it's our job to stitch together the invisible meaning of things.

And why should I bother picking up the pen when everything has already been said? No other story can ever be the father of all short stories after "Boule de Suif." I'm better off dedicating myself to love and motherhood because, after all, I am a mother.

Love is the essence of my being. And it doesn't matter how many children I will have, I'll have enough love for them all. One, two, three, four, five … and love to spare for the FatherOfMyChildren. It's possible that—at some point—my love might be divided among several men, but never between my children. Each child will have his or her own ration of infinite love every day, all the time. Three cups, a bottle of milk, and a bottomless well of love. Self-service, 24/7, free of charge. Line up and don't get impatient, there is plenty of love to go around. Can't you see? I am a woman.

Look me in the eye, Maupassant, and get something straight. I am the mother, the seamstress, the invisible gray stain, the whore. I am a huge, greasy ball of fat who has decided to sit down and write. And you're going to lift your head from your grave and hear what I have to say. We both know you must have regrets, what a waste of a life. And you'll just have two words to add: *I knew.* And with admiration, I will reply: *Rest in peace.*

NINE

Damn Little Soul-Stealers

A woman who writes is a dangerous woman. A danger to herself and a danger to others. *Be careful. Be careful.* Ever since I was a child, when at eight years old I wrote my first suicide note so that my parents would have to live with that burden forever. A foolproof punishment, except for the fact that I wouldn't have dared to die. They didn't care, they still didn't let me sleepover at my best friend's house. And I lived to tell the tale.

No woman should ever explain herself. And more importantly, no mother should ever say her piece. We all know from experience just how unbearable a mother's discourse can be. And so it's literally and literarily forbidden. Mothers and their explanations are a genre unto themselves, but they must be domestic, clandestine.

D1 is twelve months old when Elvira Lindo publishes *Lo que me queda por vivir.* During the launch, she speaks for a moment about the mother she was, a woman who "did what she could." "The years pass and my books are still on the shelves," she says at one point during the talk. And she looks at me when she says it. I'm listening in the front row, wearing a white linen dress and as young as only a woman of thirty-six holding her first baby can be. Elvira pauses and I know that she sees her younger self. I listen to everything she has to tell me. She gives me the sense that there's no rush, that there are things you can't miss and others that can wait. I can't miss my girls. What can wait are my plans, my desires, everything else.

Today, four years after that white linen dress, I know what Elvira was trying to say. And I know that she's right. The books are still on the shelves, and the new question is: but where is my head? I can't help but draw conclusions.

I used to dream of a wheat field, endless, infinite. Blue sky and golden grain. There were children playing in the dream, at the back of the scene, almost at the limit of where the eye could reach, playing on the edge of the abyss, or at the end of the world. There, at the furthest reaches of my dream. Then, two things happened: first, a black bird that wasn't a crow crossed the sky and disappeared. Then the Pink Panther crept across the scene on tiptoe.

I've always been afraid of my dreams. Until I became a mother. The day D1 was born, I stopped dreaming.

I miss it.

I remember dreaming about three deer walking in the twilight and those same animals changing into ice sculptures. I dreamed about a funeral, over and over again. My body, collapsed on a man's grave. I dreamed of the sea, the devil, a white door. I dreamed of a rubber dishwashing glove hung up on the front door to a house, inflated like a balloon.

When I was pregnant with D1, everybody warned me that I should prepare myself for sleepless nights, that children would rob me of my rest. Nobody told me that they also rob you of your dreams.

When I stopped dreaming, I knew that something had vanished, something that had always been. Externally, the change was imperceptible. But inside, I became a stranger. One's dreams are no small thing.

At first, I thought that I was still dreaming and just not remembering anything, the REM stage and all that. I wasn't worried. But time went by, too many nights without a single vision, no trace of a nightmare. I was no longer jolted awake, elated or subdued by whatever I had experienced in my dreams. And one day I realized what had happened: I had lost my soul. Although *lose* isn't quite the right word, given that I knew where it was: my daughter had devoured it.

It's hard to know who you are when your soul has been ripped to shreds. In fact, in some ways, you feel like you're not anybody at all. The soul is that hidden something inside us, according to Jung, both imperceptible and essential.

"This baby has stolen my soul." I'd heard that phrase before, but never taken it seriously. I suppose if I hadn't decided to become a mother, my soul would still be in its rightful place. The only consolation is recognizing myself in my friends' eyes. By definition, we mothers are soulless.

The loss of one's soul is a complex process; it doesn't happen overnight. A perfectly executed job, seamless, in which we actively participate. In my case, at least. Because for a while I believed, and bragged, that I had it all. I had created life in my belly and there was just one thing that I knew for sure: my body was the bridge between the concrete, human present and eternity. In other words: I was God. Worrying about the mundane (success, money, politics, war, achievement, a full night's sleep) is difficult when you're a woman who has just become a mother. With a six-month-old baby in her arms, a woman is the salt of the earth. Who could worry about sleeping at a time like that? Motherhood connected me to something bigger, better, and more powerful than myself, but it also gently wiped away my borders. It's a slow process. At first, your sharp edges are worn down, your personal obsessions, whims. A slight erasure of desire. A mother must realize that her identity is of secondary importance with respect to her child. Easy, it's easy to renounce your mortal identity when you're God. But right around the same time, your sleep is changing, your ability to meet basic needs, to work, to concentrate on any object that isn't the baby. And while the woman is being erased, the universe, life, something bigger is filling her in. Until, when at last nothing is left of who you once were, you can say to yourself: Now, I am better. I am great and power-ful. And you cry with overwhelming joy and distant pity for the woman you thought you had known.

D1 woke me every two hours, every hour, every three, every six, every half hour, every two, every eight. Every night for a whole year, every single night. This is the preparation stage. A constant assault on the uncon-scious. Nursing on demand helps shape this sort of sub-liminal and absolute surrender to the baby. The issue isn't how many hours of sleep a mother gets, it's the fact that her sleep will no longer be her own.

A mother might sleep two, three, ten hours, but the fact is that when she goes to bed she never knows what kind of tunnel awaits her, when she'll be called to action, how many pacifiers she'll replace, bottles she'll warm, cries she'll comfort, how many times she'll open her eyes against her will ... Sooner or later, a mother becomes frightened of not sleeping, scared to go to bed, scared of her own rest. It's getting late, the woman thinks before she crumples.

One of those nights, all of those nights, Man says good night, gives me a kiss, and holds me from behind. Some-times, after we've checked that D1 is breathing deep and peacefully, we make love. Then I close my eyes in the hope I'll quickly fall asleep. Time to rest, I tell myself. Hurry.

Sleep. There's no time. Relax. Think. No, relax. Book a place in the country with free cancellations. Buy red tights for D1. Rest. Report the broken hinge on the bathroom door to the home insurance company. She's going to wake up. Get tickets for the Sílvia Pérez Cruz concert.

D1 lets me sleep reasonably well after five or six months. My problem wasn't the quantity, but the quality. For years, even now, I go to bed not knowing whether or not I'll be allowed to sleep. This clearly affects one's personality, like any form of torture sustained over time.

At the park, at daycare, some mothers brag about how well their babies sleep. Anyone who has spent time in those spaces has heard something along the lines of *We slept a full six hours* or *Seven hours straight last night!* But such an intense quantification of sleep only reveals (in this and every case) that we've abandoned the essential: to sleep is not the same as to dream.

What follows is the story of a woman de-souled.

TEN

Culture and Time: A Recipe for Erasure

To be a mother is to mimic another woman. This was something I quickly realized. The problem was, I didn't know who to imitate. Long before I gave birth, I told myself the same thing we all do: I won't be like MyMother. I'm going to do it right, my son will wear a skirt, my daughter will never submit to a man, I'm going to raise a happy person. I'm going to be a *different kind of mother.*

The truth is, no matter how far you run, no matter where you arrive, you wind up imitating another woman. She doesn't have to be someone you know, she doesn't even have to share your ideology, education, or social class. To become a mother is to give birth to other women who make themselves at home, uninvited. Impossible to predict who they will be or when they will attack. In my subconscious, thousands, millions of other mothers wove what is in my heart. I'm talking about the women who gave birth before me, women and their magic bodies in the middle of the woods or deep in a cave. But I had no idea, because nobody had ever told me about them. And so, like all the women of my generation, I felt completely unprepared to be a mother, and for a very simple reason: I was unprepared.

The truth was that I had spent my young adulthood in a high-performance training regime that was preparing me for something other than motherhood. I was going to be something else.

I finished my degree with excellent grades and an

impeccable profile, went right on to a Master's program, then another, then a year in Scotland studying English (too many Spaniards in London). I got a job at exactly the right time, moved into a slightly better position at an opportune moment, had sex with as many guys as I could, and a couple of girls, too, leased my first car at twenty-six (a navy-blue Ford Focus), fell in love for real, as prescribed, bought my first apartment with Man after we had lived together for a few years ... And when the moment came to have kids, I thought there was time to spare, and money in the bank to put toward in vitro.

For us girls who follow the predictable timeline of the marketplace, the idea of motherhood strikes in our thirties, a bit earlier for the most precocious among us, a little later for the very, very busy. Sometimes the buzzer never goes off. Who needs it? We aren't obliged to become mothers. Not everyone has to be fluent in English, either, but don't forget the *is-ought* we have developed with respect to that language. One ought to study English. For getting a job, for travel, in order not to be provincial ... one *ought*. Our sense of maternal duty undergoes the same process as the language of global commerce, only it's been happening a lot longer, for millennia. An unbreachable wall. And all women, without exception, come up against our duty, what we ought to do. Duty that's been kneaded over millions of years. We eat our bread piping hot out of the oven, without stopping to think.

And yet, the women who decide not to have children don't get off scot-free, either. While we have gotten better and some have found revindication in the NoMom movement as a response to the burden of a role they have no intention of filling, we have to recognize that there's still no NoDad movement (nor will there be). The duty belongs to us and we have to create the mechanisms to deal with it. In contrast, men are born already liberated. So free that the most committed (or old-school) of them continue to spread their seed, fucking bareback every chance they get, lest we forget.

Nevertheless, motherhood is not a position we will ever list on our resume—perhaps because it's the only position we'll get without training—despite the fact that it will definitively affect our professional future. *Tick tock, tick tock.* The biological clock of the marketplace pulsing on the wrists of the most well-prepared women, the pulse of a new generation of women: professionals.

There we were. My generation's best women, maybe the best of all time. Muscles tight, skin tense, blinders carefully placed so we didn't lose focus. The gun went off, a blazing shot, echo and speed. And we took off like pureblood mares at the Epsom Derby, racing after the strollers that would hold our babies.

What a woman can't know when she hears that shot is whether there will be new goals set, whether the wheels on the stroller will lead her somewhere. We like to think so.

A young mare is beautiful. And strong. It doesn't really matter which direction she faces, or if she gallops in circles. And, it goes without saying, it doesn't really matter which jockey rides her.

But it *is* important that the best mares don't start to get anxious; that could ruin everything. That's why companies are increasingly subsidizing the process that allows their female employees to freeze their eggs and delay motherhood. The Americans were the pioneers; they've always enjoyed putting a price on the body and all its parts. Facebook was the first company to underwrite this whim, just as modern as they are opportunistic. Then came Google, Yahoo, Uber, Spotify, and Apple. They do it to relieve their employees of the weight of their duty; women aren't just paying to freeze their genetic material, but to get the damn obligation of motherhood off their backs.

"Can someone tell me how much it costs to not have to think about this anymore?" a young woman asks as she waits in line at the movies. Her date, who will cease to interest her after a few nights, has just bought the popcorn.

"I'm prepared to pay, too. My company will pay, my parents will help," begs another woman, a thirty-seven-year-old lawyer.

"Just tell me where to sign," another says. She's wealthy. She doesn't care about the price, just whether or not it hurts. "I don't want to waste time thinking about this right now," she urgently declares.

Don't worry, don't be afraid, soothes the white coat at the fertility clinic. Your money will buy you time. And if you haven't got enough cash up front, we can set up easy payments once you've given us your most recent pay stubs from your job as a lawyer, economist, professor, technical engineer, computer programmer ...

But professions, resumes, and other falsehoods surrounding female identity aside, the truth is that I invested a lot—like many women of my generation—in making the most of time, not wasting it, achieving my goals as quickly as possible. And then all of a sudden, from one day to the next, a baby appeared and all the clocks shattered. Forever.

Say goodbye to your precious efficiency when you're rocking a newborn. Productivity just doesn't jibe with the tempo of love. Love is an idyllic interval, a moment in time when you take off your watch. It's also the only time no one has managed to get paid for yet, which doesn't necessarily make it better.

That was the point of rupture, I think. From the time she was born, D1 was an energy vacuum. She destroyed every single one of my routines until all my time became the baby's time. For many months, we had three major (and exclusive) occupations: eat, sleep, cry.

Living can be very sad. We create meaning from our days with a web of routine and lies. And this makes us sad. It would make anybody sad. We know the future is unpredictable and that we have as much control over our lives as a dinosaur over the fate of its species. But the bills come each month and we've made the decision to love and respect each other. And so I suppose it seems like the real thing. Life.

When my first daughter was born, my life finally gained a new sense of meaning. That day, all the living and all the dead inhabiting this planet looked me in the eye simultaneously and said:

"Nice to have you here."

"I'm the happiest woman on earth," I replied.

There was a long silence. A silence that lasted for months, years. Until one day, all the living and all the dead inhabiting this planet finally answered:

"It will be nice when you're gone."

"I'm nobody," I answered charitably.

Sleep, eat, cry. The meaning of the ocean is the ocean itself, not the sum of its drops. I could die, or I could simply be her mother. And it might not even matter.

But it's way too soon for that. D1 has just been born and everyone has come to see us in the hospital. The room is filled with people who love me and who love her as soon as they set eyes on her. They love her even more than they love me. They give her the love they didn't know how to give me, the love I didn't have time to accept, the love I never knew existed. And now, it all belongs to her.

ELEVEN

Entrance Exam

I try to feed D1 with too many people around. It's hard. I can't figure out whether or not she's gotten anything. All I know is that it hurts. My nipple doesn't stick out as far as it should.

The midwife brings me to a nursing room first thing and explains how to nurse. She touches my breasts and shows me how the colostrum (the serous liquid that precedes milk in mammals) comes out when I squeeze a little. You have to make a sort of scissor shape with your fingers and grip the nipple in the center and then the baby can latch on. The midwife's cold hands make me feel like my breasts could be anyone's. I don't like it.

"That baby is hungry," MyMother says. "You could stop fiddling with your boobs and give her a bottle."

I don't know what to do. I have no idea what I should do. So I do nothing. I just cradle D1 in my arms and stroke her cheek as she cries, pressed against my breast, which has been naked and at the ready since she arrived thirty-two hours ago. My nipple rests just above her nose. I don't try to get her to latch or to eat. I expect nothing, nothing happens. Just three tears of milk that leak out and slip slowly down my skin until they brush D1's parted lips. And that's how it happens. I feed her little bird's mouth for the first time.

My hungry daughter in my arms, I realize I've never seen how a baby actually nurses. And if I had, I certainly hadn't paid attention.

"You'll need to give her a bottle after every feeding," the pediatrician says as we leave. "She's already lost more than a pound and needs to gain weight." Then she writes *mixed feeding* on D1's chart and repeats that we are not to skip a single bottle.

Formula is white, abundant, fatty, and delicious, and I'm still releasing that paltry, yellowish concoction. But I know breastfeeding is a natural process that should not be interfered with. And much less with formula. I've read that without breastfeeding "bonding can be a challenge" and my friends have confirmed it. "The bond" is the union between mother and child. When they say bonding can be "a challenge" if you don't nurse, what they mean is that you love your child less.

I'm going to do it right. It doesn't matter that D1 cries day and night. It doesn't matter that my breasts are raw, nipples cracked. Who cares if I bleed a bit at the start of every feeding, a little sip of blood won't hurt her, it only hurts me. All that matters is keeping track of how much D1 pees, and that she is peeing. Her diaper has to be nice and wet in order to confirm that my daughter isn't dehydrated. I'm prepared to starve her before being accused of loving her any less. That's why I ignore the pediatrician.

I don't give her a single bottle. We go home on Friday and there's no doctor in the office until Monday. Just the emergency room. Forty-eight hours and counting. I don't reveal to anyone that I'm disobeying orders.

The goal isn't simply for the baby to eat and grow, formula is just as good for that. The truth is that breast milk serves other, much more important functions. On the one hand, it promises the fusion of mother and child, the test we all want to pass. And on the other, it has been deemed the very best nourishment possible for a human baby. And parents want the best at any price.

A perfect recipe: two scoops of the marketplace, three scoops of mysticism, and one best mother in the world. Mix, shake, and heat.

Years later, I'll click through the American website onlythebreast.com, where pictures of rosy infants are interspersed with images of carefully marked bags of breast milk: "non-smoker," "100% organic," "26 years old. Vegan. Athlete." 230 milliliters cost about 14 euros. A two-month-old baby might drink about five bottles of that amount per day. In other words, 2,100 euros of breast milk a month, down the hatch.

Nature becomes unnatural when you start to hear coins jingle, as threatening as the sound of spent shells from a rifle. But that's the marketplace, always hungry: gay couples, mothers via surrogacy, athletes who put it in their protein shakes, parents who want to stimulate their children's immune systems ... they all want the best. There's even a service for wet nurses to come to your home and nurse for 885 euros a week (plus a 4,450-euro deposit and accommodation for the wet nurse and her own child).

The coins jingle and the milk that is sold is often mixed. The suppliers—the mothers—behave like actual dealers and have learned to cut their product with cow's milk: they might be young, healthy, non-smoking vegans, but that doesn't mean they don't need the money.

But right now D1 is a newborn, we haven't taken her out of the apartment yet, I've never seen that website, and I haven't started to write this book. All that's happened up to this point is that we've survived our first forty-eight hours home from the hospital and I'm on my way to the health center in secret.

I burst into tears as soon as I sit down in the waiting room. I know that I've done something horrible and must confess. But I've gone mute, incapable of speech. I can only cry silently for the two hours I have to sit there. I'm still crying when I'm finally in front of the doctor.

"There's no rush," she says.

She must be over sixty. She's wearing a white coat, a little figure dressed as a doctor sewn on the lapel. Her office is filled with drawings that her young patients must have done for her. Outside, the waiting room is just as jam-packed as when I arrived.

"I've skimped on bottles," I confess. "Even though she's hungry. She's always hungry, she's hungry all the time. She's insatiable."

"You have a beautiful baby," she replies.

"She weighed just over eight pounds when she born, but since I started nursing her, she's lost a pound in two days. The doctor told me I could take her home but that I had to supplement with a bottle after every feeding. She told me not to skimp, that the baby could get dehydrated. But I haven't given her a single bottle. I have sores on my nipples and no idea how much she weighs now. She pees all the time, though. So she isn't dehydrated, I don't think ..."

"The baby is fine," the doctor assures me.

"How do you know? You haven't even weighed her."

"I know because I'm looking at her mother."

"But ... I skipped bottles."

"That's because she hasn't needed them. No one knows what is good for her better than you do. Not even the doctor at the hospital. Not even me."

"What do I do now?"

"Rest a little, for starters."

"But we need to weigh her first."

"We'll weigh her tomorrow, when we're a little calmer. I'm here every day, but you don't need instructions for how to take care of her."

"So, should I be supplementing with formula or not?"

"Give it to her when you think she needs it. Sometimes it's useful during the first weeks. Even as long as breast-feeding lasts, if necessary."

"And she won't reject me afterward?"

"Absolutely not," she smiles.

She strokes D1's tiny head. D1 won't reject anything of mine.

"Thank you," I reply.

And I know that the doctor has just explained everything I need to know, now and going forward.

The only thing she hasn't explained is where my mania to breastfeed at any cost comes from. Because at that time, I don't know that there's a website trafficking breast milk, or that many cancer patients refer to it as "white gold" because of its benefits in their fight against disease.

When I leave the health center with D1 in my arms, I'm not aware of breastfeeding's symbolic significance. I've never thought about it, nor has anyone discussed it with me. Like many women, I simply resign myself to suffering the side effects of my ignorance.

Outside, I run into a woman I know from the neighborhood, also a mom. I tell her all about what happened, sparing no details, as if she were really my friend (which she's not). I speak with the precision I've only seen used by mothers, an exacting, surgical rigor they add to the everyday.

"You did the right thing," she pronounces. "Don't give up on the breast. It's the best for both of you."

"Well, we'll see how it goes," I say.

And I think that's what will be best for us both, not having expectations. But I don't say that to the other woman.

"I had trouble with nursing at first, everyone does," my neighbor says. "But it changed my life. I discovered my true nature."

It happens instantly. Short circuit, rejection, nausea. I hear the word *nature* associated with my female body in some way and know I'm in danger. I turn my head, a gazelle looking for the concealed sharpshooter. But there's no one there, just the quiet comings and goings of the city street. Even though I suspect that, hiding somewhere behind my own shadow, a monster lies in wait, ready to devour me.

TWELVE

A Word of Warning, Mammal Mothers

Women in Africa know how to use it, and it's how Andean women carry their kids. Women who work with their children on their backs, the child integrated into the rhythm of their days, their lives. But I'm clueless about how to use the gigantic piece of organic cotton cloth that I paid a hundred euros for online when I was eight months pregnant. Right now, I'm enjoying maternity leave paid for by the state, a time in which I can dedicate myself exclusively to playing house, because the truth is that I'm not going to integrate my daughters into my routine or work like this. But I will wear the same shawl worn by women who don't have maternity leave, many of whom didn't go to university, and who ease their off-spring into their daily lives. I'm really not sure if I'm wearing the wrap in homage, as an aspirational gesture, or if it's a total farce. Fashion dictates that the baby will be more comfortable in the wrap, as explained by the CD which comes with the baby carrier, as well as the hundreds of YouTube tutorials where dozens of urban mothers purposely imitate women who live, literally, saddled with their infants. The only momentary relief I get is the knowledge that I'm not the only one: no one knows how the hell to put on this thing. MyMother, who is spending a few days with us, doesn't have the faintest idea either.

"Everything is different these days," she says.

Which, in her language, means: *You have it so much easier than I did and yet you insist on this nonsense. You must have your reasons …*

But I don't. I have no idea why I'm doing it, honestly. I don't even know *what* I'm doing. And I have no idea how to respond to MyMother.

I feel a little ridiculous watching the video. Hailed as the most natural way to carry D1, I have to admit it seems pretty artificial to be learning alone in my living room, pausing the DVD so as not to miss the instructions. I won't give up until I finally have a baby hanging from me there in the middle of our apartment, with nowhere to go and not an ounce of naturalness about me.

When a mother realizes she isn't adequately prepared to raise a child (or at least not as prepared as she would like to be), she goes looking for guides. The most modern of these guides is called "natural parenting," which is an expression used by urban mothers like me who are unfamiliar with babies and/or children. The larger the urban environment, the more alone the mother feels and the more she will defend a type of nature that's already a lost cause.

Some women start this journey even before they go into labor. They change their diet and habits during pregnancy and won't shut up about "natural birth," as if it were the latest Netflix series. The most committed among them even forgo the hospital entirely, daring to give birth on their own, in their apartment building with elevator and concierge and garage and a midwife who charges by the hour. Or they decide to abandon apartment living and opt for a housing development outside the city, or even a home in the country. Leaving the city becomes a goal, a turning point. A return we stumble toward, by fits and starts, even when we don't know to where it is we want to go back, or to which place we're trying to escape.

"Honey, maybe we should think about moving to a small town, leaving all this."

An inevitable suggestion when one has children in a big city. Sooner or later, it comes up.

"What about the girls?" Man replies.

"I'm talking about the girls," I clarify.

"Well, I'm talking about them, too. Towns aren't the opposite of the city, they aren't a cure-all for the things that bother you about living here. Small towns are the exact reason everyone chooses to live in cities. Maybe we're all wrong, or maybe small towns really are hell. I grew up in a town, you know. And I'll never go back to one. It's the worst thing that can happen to a kid, I know from experience. I will not allow you to move my daughters to a place like that."

I like the way he says *my daughters*. It makes Man sound like a woman.

"But it's so hard for them in the city. D2's stroller doesn't fit between the cars, her day care looks like a garage; it's too far to walk to D1's school, there are cigarette butts on the ground. It takes so long to do everything. I feel like I never have enough time for them."

"So we'll smash all the clocks," Man says.

He puts his arms around my waist and kisses me and runs after the children, leaving me behind. And I concede. Man is very effective when it comes to shutting me up with a kiss. I should think more about this fact.

In my case, neither birth was natural. C-sections for both. But I didn't feel an unnatural separation in either case; on the contrary, I remember the man dressed in blue scrubs who opened my womb and pulled D1 out safe and sound and put her in my arms. The doctor who took out D2 wore green and smiled as he watched her arrive.

Maybe this is why I take D1 out of the damn rag and lay her carefully in her bassinet. She likes sleeping by the window, I think. She's so pretty. Everything she is wearing was hand-sewn by friends or family. For the time being, we have nothing to fear. Moreover, I feel strong, really strong. If someone tried to hurt her, I'd rip off their arm, probably with my teeth. A lot more has been said about wolf-men than wolf-mothers, but here I am, ready to lick my cub and ready to snarl. I pace around her crib the way I've seen wild animals do in the zoo: vigilant, attentive to the constant threats that now surround us, always.

"It's natural. We're mammals," Marta says. She's my best friend and a mother of two.

She explains what co-sleeping is all about as we jog in the park. Squashed between her husband and kids, it sounds like Marta gets no sleep at all.

"What the hell are you talking about?" I have to admit, I feel better about loving nature than being classified within it. "Why do people always say things like that? Talking to parents at daycare is like reading a *National Geographic* article ..."

"That's because motherhood takes us back to our real nature. We're mammals. We nurse, we live in packs, we raise our young together."

"So that's why the four of you sleep in the same bed?"

"And you sleep alone, do you?" Marta accuses me.

"No, I sleep with Man."

"Well, your baby doesn't like sleeping by herself, either. It's unnatural. Mammals don't sleep alone," she pronounces.

"Mammals don't sleep alone," I repeat, worried.

For another half an hour, Marta and I run in silence through Madrid's Casa del Campo in our thermal mammal leggings. In amongst the trees, I can make out other women with thigh-high patent leather boots, selling sex to men who will pay for it. Those women must be a product of culture, and we mammal-mothers the product of nature. Or maybe it's the opposite. It rained earlier, and my sneakers sink into the damp earth with each stride. I wonder which is more immoral, nature or culture.

As we continue our run, I repeat three words to myself, again and again, in time with my breath, increasingly ragged: "I am a woman, I am a woman, I am a woman, I am a woman, I am a woman ..."

Since I had a baby, many of my friends, acquaintances, and even just other women—strangers— who happen to be raising children want to talk to me about "my nature" and "what's natural" and "the fact that we're mammals." And it's scary every time, it's as if someone wanted to shut me away in a barn. There are domesticated animals, and there are wild ones. When they say *mammal*, I sense they're referring to domesticated females of the species. Women put someplace comfortable, cushy, with Wi-Fi and vegan meals; somewhere we should get away from, and fast. That's the best-case scenario. What's much worse are the two thousand mammal farms in India where women acting as surrogates are housed like animals and serve two functions only: eat and reproduce.

The market is incredibly flexible when it comes to buying women's bodies by the hour, or month, or even in pieces. By contrast, the market is much more conservative when doing business with unisex body parts. You can't sell blood or kidneys, only donate them. But you can buy breast milk, and uteruses can be rented for nine irreversible months.

And yet, the expression "rent-a-womb" is a just a euphemism. What is in fact being rented is a mother. More than one part of a woman is used in procreation. Everything a woman is and everything that transcends her is used to create new life from her flesh and bones.

And this is something any woman who has planted a couple of embryos in her belly knows well. The embryo isn't enough, the uterus isn't enough. You need a mother. And we owe them our lives, all those mothers who decided to give birth and will decide to do so in the future. And yet the market is so creative that a woman who rents her womb can also give up her parental rights to the child she will bear. She can even renounce the child's right to know her, the mother who bore him or her. It's all dangerously arranged so that, with respect to women, to the surrogates, anything can be bought for whatever price the consumer is willing to pay.

We women often try to escape culture because culture is misogynistic, the consumer-goods marketplace has us beat with its enormous pressure of supply and demand on our bodies, and the labor market has determined that we are destined to earn less than a man is for the same work. But mother nature is a trap, too. Of the two options, sometimes I think that a woman in search of her true nature might have it worse.

I've picked up on a trail since becoming a mother; it could be the scent of blood dripping from prey, or a caramel-covered apple at the carnival I'm about to enter. Impossible to know because I can't find a single bread-crumb or any other way to go back. Only the future, only misinterpretations. Today, I'm sure of just one thing: each one of us must travel every inch of the road on her own.

THIRTEEN

A Mother Is

D1 must have been five months old when I thought about my own birth for the first time since becoming a mother. I wasn't alone on the day I was born; there is always at least one woman with us when we arrive. The woman that we scratch and scrape to make our way out: with our head, our rump, an elbow, our toes.

When I was young, I imagined that the occasion of my birth had been a party and MyMother an elegant hostess in a nightgown. A grand day for her, the day I was born. But now I also know that I had to break her to get out. Of course, I had known about the process since I was eight or nine. But now I understand it differently, through time and flesh.

Until I became a mother, I wasn't completely MyMother's daughter.

"Being a mother will change your life." That's what everyone told me when I got pregnant the first time. And so I tried to imagine what kind of future awaited me after giving birth. But I was mistaken. Motherhood changed my *past*, it was a new way to perceive all that had happened before. How could becoming a mother change my life in an instant if it didn't also modify everything that came first? The truth is, nothing and nobody will change your life if they can't change your memory.

Somehow, giving birth is the best way to understand just how much love it took to get you here. And to elevate to their rightful place all the women who have done it before you.

In my case, the woman that gave birth to me is the same one that raised me. Maybe that's why I never gave the slightest importance to the fact that I came out of MyMother's womb. And yet, I know now that they could have been two different people, MyBirthMother and the MotherThatRaisedMe, and if so I would have loved each of them differently. That's why I think about MyMother so many nights. I think about going to the home where she has long lived as a widow and giving her all I have.

MyMother has a green aluminum mailbox, and on it a gold plaque bearing her name. And below her name: *Widow of* + my father's last name. Every time I go to her house, I see that plaque and I regret everything I've done; I feel like the worst daughter in the world and I want to go back in time and hug her and be nothing but good to her for the rest of my life.

But I always visit MyMother on the wrong days. Today, for example, I've turned up in her kitchen because my grandmother (her mother) is dying. The doctors have said that she won't make it out of the hospital, but I know she will. She always does. But because I also know that it will have to happen sooner or later, I've come home, like I always do when my grandmother is preparing herself to die.

So here I am, perched like a lizard on the tile floor I've watched MyMother mop countless times. And from this position, I realize that when she dies I'll be left with the absence only a mother's death can provide. I watch her, knowing we are linked by that abyss, that we build it between the two of us. It's an abyss we widen with every step, a path we must walk to link one life to another, one death to another. And this is how time is stitched and sewn. I am in that abyss now, and what's more, it is the best possible place.

Her back to me, MyMother washes last night's dishes. The water is running and the kitchen smells like coffee.

"This detergent is wonderful," she says. "My hands are so much nicer since I started using it. It must be true, what they say in the commercials."

"Your hands are the softest hands I have ever felt in my life, mamá. They don't need any advertisement."

I watch her scrub away at the bottom of a frying pan. I like watching her work because MyMother has always given her full attention to everything she does, ever since I can remember. For many years, she put her hands on me that way, with the same efficacy that polishes the pan. I see MyMother's hands smoothing sunscreen on my cheeks, washing the floor that is now beneath my feet, tying the ribbon in my hair, wrapping my Christmas presents, washing the box where I kept my turtles, checking my hair for lice, buttoning my smock, wiping my nose, paying for our tickets to the circus, cleaning a scrape. I go to her then, take her hands from the sink and bring them to my face so I can feel them on my cheeks again, so I can kiss them.

She waves me off.

"What are you doing? Look! The floor is getting soaked! Go on now, dry that face and drink your coffee."

FOURTEEN

MyMother's Mother

My grandmother's arms are black and blue (marks left by the spikes in her blood sugar), her bones are razor sharp under the skin, flesh sags from her midsection, the backs of her arms, her breasts; she wears diapers, can't walk, needs a straw to drink. She pants before every word. I used to not know what to do when she got sick, in her other brushes with death: I only watched her and spoke to her. I used to think that this was what a dying person needed, an opportunity for last words. A farewell, a chance to say their regrets, perhaps; I felt it was generous to cede them the word, in the mystery of the end. But dying actually looks a lot more like being born than I would have thought. It would be just as odd for someone in the throes of death to deliver a big speech as if one of my babies had spoken to me in the operating room.

Luckily, I'm already a mother when my grandmother really is about to die. I've witnessed birth. And I'm ready to be with her as she goes. I'm not expecting her final words, I don't expect words at all. I don't have to speak to make my presence known, which is a real achievement for me.

Instead, I massage her arms with calendula oil. I carry it in my purse because I massage D1 when she has gas. I sing quietly so MyMother's mother can fall asleep, I hold her hand on the white Formica of the hospital tray table, I count out loud the drips in the hanging bag of antibiotics, I explain what the women are arguing about on TV at

5 p.m. and assess who is right: it appears the chubbier one slept with the blonder one's husband. Sometimes I brush what little hair she still has, as if she were a doll. I spritz her with eau de cologne. And at some point—if everything has gone well—she falls asleep.

Caring for my grandmother at night was made more bearable thanks to psychologist Penelope Leach's action protocol for dealing with a colicky infant. Leach is the author of a thousand-page manual on caring for babies and children, a true gem, in which she explains, among other things, what to do in the event of colic. A recipe that turns out to be just as effective for colic as for death itself.

Colic is when a two-month-old baby cries uninterrupted for three to five hours, as if they were exploding in pain. Their hands and feet go rigid and they stretch out their arms as if they were about to break. It usually starts in the late afternoon, when the mother is at her most tired and banking on the baby falling asleep. No one is sure why colic occurs, or why it disappears. For such situations, Penelope Leach developed ten steps to follow: a series of massages, walks, leg exercises, food, water. Clear guidelines for each step. And then Step Ten, the most important of all, in which Leach states that, if nothing you've tried has helped, the colic must not be present. Otherwise, she suggests starting over from the beginning.

The night my grandmother is dying in front of me, I methodically follow the steps for easing colic because I know that at some point Step Ten will come: the pain will let up, or she'll go. And if she's still here, a possibility I'm beginning to consider increasingly remote, I can always start back at Step One. I don't have to be afraid, I just have to follow the steps.

At three o'clock in the morning, she starts moaning quietly, grinding her agony between her teeth with each breath and looking at me as though it's all my fault. By four she doesn't remember my name; I could be one of her daughters, I could be her neighbor, she can't recall. I tell her that I can call the nurse if she starts to get too uncomfortable. Then she recognizes me again.

"Stop with that nonsense," she says. "Can't you see they're all going to be here soon? They're spending the night and the house is a disaster! You should be making the beds instead of staring at me like an idiot."

"Look at me, Grandma. I'm here."

"Why are you looking at me like that? They're about to arrive! Don't just stand there! I can't understand why you're so lazy. Honestly, you were born lazy. I've never seen you make a bed in your entire life. I'm going to die before I ever see you make a bed. You don't even seem like a woman. And don't look at me like that: you ought to be ashamed."

Just when I think she's about to spit in my face, she starts wheezing again. She can't talk while dying.

My grandmother thinks we're alone. She doesn't see her roommate, a solitary old woman. The hospital beds are too close together for the family member who has to sit between them. Me, in this case. Nobody sits with the other woman, the three of us are alone, although my grandmother doesn't take her neighbor into account. She stares at the light shining through the half-open door on the opposite side of the room. She's obsessed with the strip of brightness that leads out to the hallway on the 11th floor, Pulmonology.

"I'm not going to say it again. Can you please shut that door?"

"I think we better keep it open, Grandma. I can't turn off the lights in the hall."

"My children are asleep in the next room and the light bothers them. You're oblivious, you know they're tired and the light bothers them, is it really so hard to close the door? You'll never find a husband who will put up with you."

"We're not at home, Grandma. I can't turn off the light."

"Forget it, I'll do it myself. Better than sending you. Some woman you are."

She turns away so she doesn't have to look at me.

My grandmother has never treated me like this. She has never in her entire life put her expectations on me (or any of her children). Not until now, the very night we have to say goodbye to each other.

I'm worried about MyMother and what's about to happen. There's a part in the Joyce Carol Oates novel *Mother Missing* that details what's to come with tremendous clarity: *Something ruptured and began bleeding in my chest when I bent over my mother, when I saw my mother in that way. It will happen to you, in a way special to you. You will not anticipate it, you cannot prepare for it, and you cannot escape it. The bleeding will not cease for a long time.* That passage frightened me, its threat and certainty. But MyMother hasn't read Oates. MyMother hasn't read almost any of the books I have, and probably not a single one of the books that changed my life. But my grandmother will die anyway.

It's clearly a matter of life or death at the moment. And yet, I have no desire to make the beds. My grandmother will have to die with that knowledge.

She never asks the nurses to leave the room or talks to them about her visitors. I've come to think that she's losing her mind, but that's not it. Whatever it is that's happening, it will come for all of us. Nobody escapes. The light that creeps under the door and doesn't stop. "How many times must I tell you to close it?" I had never prayed for dawn before that night. Eventually, my grandmother settles for me promising to make the beds, and rests at last.

It's six o'clock in the morning. We are victorious. She sleeps, her mouth open and round like a full moon. When she wakes a few hours later, her gestures remind me of D1. Not just because they've removed her dentures, and she has—like the baby—a half toothless smile. It's also in the way she furrows her brow so seriously and how she passes from fury to tenderness with only a brief flutter at the corner of her mouth. Not to mention her eyes, so alive, identical in both the elderly woman and the baby. I don't know whether the little life she has left is escaping by way of her gaze, or if all her energy is focused on keeping it in there, trapped.

This morning, as she moaned with pain and pressed her thumb on the damn button the nurses don't even bother getting up for anymore, she took a breath and said: "You're so beautiful." Her eyes are small, no lashes left to bat in farewell. "How old are you?"

"Thirty-six."

"You're just a girl. Do you have children?"

"A daughter, D1."

She closed her eyes then, as if nothing hurt.

Not as long as there were little girls.

FIFTEEN

The Surrender to MyMother

My grandmother was poor. MyMother got pregnant unexpectedly, too young at twenty. She wore white when she married, and a wide-brimmed tulle hat. She had the most delicate face I've ever seen. In the pictures, she looks like a ceramic Lladró figurine in the hands of a child.

Long before that, my grandmother gave birth to MyMother, also when she was young, also unplanned. I think it's quite possible that my grandmother almost didn't have MyMother. I think she knew perfectly well how to get rid of a pregnancy.

MyMother remembers that when she was six, a very elegant couple came to have tea with them. MyMother wore a red coat and a pair of winter shoes two sizes too big, the same ones she would wear for the next three winters. But the couple didn't take MyMother home with them. Instead, my grandmother sent her off to a public boarding school for six months. A place where she was fed three times a day, every day. And where she learned to write her name. They slept on old, worn sheets so thin they would rip when you looked at them, according to MyMother. Once, one of the nuns sat my mother down in the stone courtyard and tried to make her mend the tear. MyMother didn't know how to sew. The nun locked her in a windowless room as punishment, so she would learn. But she never did. The nun said she was stubborn, that she didn't want to learn. And she was right, MyMother didn't.

My grandmother didn't like to talk about her children. She had eight of them. One died during childbirth and another after just ten days of life. Six made it. MyMother was the first. She loved children, my grandmother did. Or at least that's how it seemed to me, her granddaughter. She liked to play with me and buy me presents. But she didn't like when we women had babies at the wrong time.

"You always have your children on your own," she would say.

"Well, I might need a man to help make them, Grandma," I joked.

"I hear a lot of nonsense nowadays. All this guff about men being able to help."

"Maybe that's because they can."

"Don't be a fool. Children belong to their mother."

MyMother was my grandmother's daughter. And my grandmother decided to have her. And she decided to raise her at home with her five siblings. She decided to raise all of her children even though they'd have to wear shoes that were two sizes too big. My grandfather, apparently, wasn't much help.

When MyMother got married, she went far away to live with my father, the man that was to give her me, one of those children that "belong to their mother." Shortly thereafter, I became very ill. I was six months old with a fever that wouldn't break. It was very cold in the apartment where we lived. My parents had no heat, no woodstove, no fireplace, and not much money. MyMother stuck me between her breasts and I kept on burning beneath the cold sheets. MyMother thought I was dying. So she called my grandmother from a phone booth, a fistful of coins held tightly in her hand.

"I don't know what to do, mamá. I think the baby is dying."

"*Hija de puta*, that's what you get for leaving home."
And she hung up.

Years later, we went on vacation together: my grandmother, MyMother, and me. My father had died by then, one night without warning. The hotel had a huge swimming pool.

In an airport shop, my grandmother bought me a doll. An expensive one. My Tender Darling, that's what the doll was called. It was the size of a real baby.

"Mamá! What are you doing? We just got here—why are you spending so much at the start of the vacation?" MyMother said.

"Because *we're on vacation*. I don't want to end up without enough time to spend some money."

I understood what she meant.

My grandmother is the strongest woman I ever knew.

When MyMother told me about my fever and how close I'd been to death, my grandmother's insult, her cruelty, was seared in my mind. I still carry the scar from that wound. I was fifteen years old then, and was always asking MyMother about each and every event in her life—which was my life, too. I didn't speak to my grandmother for three months, although I'd swear she never even noticed my silence. But it would take years, many more years, for me to reach the conclusion—just before her death—that my grandmother wasn't cruel.

I needed to outlive her in order to understand her pain and exhaustion after eight children, after two dead babies. And a daughter who didn't learn, who didn't want to.

Thanks to that daughter, we're here today.

All her life, MyMother's mother was too tired for her. And now when MyMother needs me most, when she's puddled in sorrow on the hospital floor, I can't pick her up, either.

SIXTEEN

Violently

We pay four euros per word for the first ten words with which we announce my grandmother's death in the obituary pages of the provincial newspaper. Fifty cents for each additional word until we reach the thirty-five words we've chosen as her farewell. That was the only time in her life that my grandmother's name appeared in the press. She wasn't a socially relevant woman, she was seventy-four, she had been sick a long time, it was a grief expected and accepted by those of us who mourned her. But it left everything a little tighter: our skirts a size smaller and our hearts in a corset.

My grandmother never saw me make a bed. It was one of her final wishes before she died. And she died without witnessing it.

D1 was six months old when my grandmother died. D2 hadn't been born yet, but I already knew that my grandmother was leaving without meeting someone important.

I understand why some people detest children or the elderly or both. It's their damn insistence. You can't get them to shut up; they make noise even when they're not saying anything. Why am I here? What's happened to me? Who are you, and why are you here with me? Those eyes that say: *I love you, don't go, I need you, I love you so much, I need you so badly, will I always need you like this?* Love, leaking from their eyes, that sweet, heady stink. Eyes that love, that love you and need you even to breathe.

Children and the elderly have an enormous capacity for gratitude only proportional to their capacity for demand. But there are people who don't like to feel loved in such an overwhelming way. They fear they can't love enough in return. Which is normal, because they can't. It's hard not to look away from someone who is about to leave this world, just as it's hard to hold a newborn who is seeing for the first time. Both travel through time, both are coming or going. That's why many mothers "fall in love" with their babies, because those babies pass through them for the first time, as if neither love nor time had even existed before. And it's the reason it is so difficult to say goodbye to someone we love. Even in their final breath, we want to give them more. We want to receive more. Even if it is more pain.

MyMother held my grandmother's hand just before she died, she heard her take her last breath in the adjustable hospital bed, in a box surrounded by plastic curtains.

"Go ahead, we don't want her to suffer," she said to the physician on call.

After that night, MyMother has heard that same breath on other occasions. In truth, she's carried that breath in her chest ever since. I know she still chokes on the sorrow that arrives in the middle of the afternoon out of nowhere, assaulting her while she waits in line at the butcher shop, repeating "a pound of sirloin steaks" to herself. And later, she feels her mother's cold hand when she squeezes my warm one, at the movies or on the couch. A new pain nests inside MyMother, pulses within her like a heartbeat. We could probably measure it with a Doppler. Just like when I saw D1 and D2's hearts for the first time.

"Can you hear it?" the doctor asked me. "It's alive. Your baby is fine. It's still here."

Those little seeds of a heart sounded like the thunder of a galloping horse. Before, I had heard the muffled nothing of hearts that hadn't stayed with me. It's the same with a dead mother. She remains inside of us, nestled in the hollow our children made, the children we had and those we didn't. The fact is, she stays there. Someday, they'll invent a next-generation Doppler that will detect the heartbeats of the dead we carry inside. It will be manufactured in China, they'll call it Angel Sound, it will cost between a hundred and two hundred euros, we'll buy it on Amazon Prime (these sorts of things are always bought in a hurry). Then we will listen to the gallop of the dead inside us until, one day, they go quiet and all that's left is silence.

Although we unfortunately don't have access to an Angel Sound yet, I can feel MyMother's pain radiating outward. I can plunge my hands into that pain just like I can plunge them into the batter for the cake we keep baking with my grandmother's recipe: one lemon yogurt, two yogurt containers of flour, two of oil, two of sugar, three eggs, a tablespoon of baking powder. It's a sticky pain that stains everything it touches. At this very moment, it's even dirtying the red flowers on D1's embroidered shirt. D1 is sitting on the floor in front of me. She's coloring silently, which is how she needs to be when Mamá is writing. Only Mamá isn't writing just now. Just now, Mamá is watching her. She loves to color. She draws a princess with a long dress made of flower petals, each petal a different color, like a rainbow. The red flowers on her shirt are so bright they almost blind me.

Sometimes MyMother feels bad that, in the end, my grandmother had to die in the hospital, in an anonymous bed surrounded by plastic curtains. But that isn't really how it was: as far as my grandmother was concerned, she died in a house with open windows and unmade beds—guests were on their way and she was angry that I didn't want to make them. May she rest in peace.

Shortly after my grandmother dies, Chantal Maillard publishes *La mujer de pie* (Woman on Foot), a book about a mother's death. "I don't want you to go, not completely. But the truth is that you are disappearing-in-me and this is what hurts, that absent being, that becoming absent, or perhaps the idea of absence that accompanies your image. Diluted, when I wanted to trap it." Chantal is right. She explains that a mother has just died violently inside her daughters, just as we are born violently through them. For months, the mother's body shelters those who are yet to come. And in doing so, that mother prepares herself to hold those that are yet to die. She'll hold them for months, even years. Our mothers will dissolve in us just as our children formed within.

It's good to think about these things. These thoughts can be the stilts on which we build our dwelling over water after a shipwreck. A rudimentary—maybe even useless—construction, where water leaks when it rains; but still, it's a roof we can huddle under. It could end up being my only shelter. MyMother doesn't think about these things.

SEVENTEEN

My Name Is Lucy

There's a time, usually in the evening when the sun is just about to set, in which a mother is the woman waiting by the window. She's waiting for a man and, as she does, she quietly celebrates that she has everything she wants, even though this damn waiting could ruin it all. And then the woman stares. Through that window. For a long time. None of us wants to sit before that emptiness. The windowsill where the self-sacrificing mother of yore set her exhaustion down. The frame through which we will watch our children leave when they abandon us. And yet, this window also belongs to the world's best mother. The mother who puts her children—naturally—above her desires. The mother who questions nothing and whose capacity for love is more important than anything else. More important than herself.

This afternoon, I am that mother. I'm alone and looking from our balcony in La Latina, in Madrid, and I know that I'll watch my life pass by through this glass. The day might even arrive when, if I pay close enough attention, I'll see it return.

The truth is I don't really believe I am alone in the world, that much is clear. For example, I sense the nearby hand—almost so close I could touch it—of a mother my age watering plants on her small balcony in Brooklyn Heights. I also feel the hands that baked cakes in the 1960s suburbs, not so long ago. And I'm about to ask that other mother—the one sitting on a terrace in the bustle of a Rio favela—to roll me a cigarette. We all have something in common: a mother raising a child becomes, sooner or later, a woman that waits inside a house.

And though I'm obviously not alone, I can't really talk about this with anyone. This is another kind of loneliness. Unless, I don't know, the phone would ring; something I can make happen at this very moment. Because right here and now, I'm in charge, and what I feel like making happen can happen. And whomever I want can call.

"Hi. Can you talk?" The voice is thick, ancient.

"Just while the baby's sleeping. Who are you?"

"Lucy."

"Sorry, I think you have the wrong number."

"That's impossible. I'm calling because you just asked me to."

"Lucy ... Lucy who?"

"Just Lucy. I'm the Mother of Mankind, we know each other."

"Okay, sure."

"Google it if you don't believe me. Or better yet, try to remember. African, Ethiopia, short stature, three foot seven, sixty-four pounds, mother of a number of children, I don't remember how many, you've seen me on TV."

"How old are you?"

"Hard to say. I've been on the planet for three million years already. But I died around age twenty, and my mind is intact, the same as then. So actually, I'm younger than you."

"I'm talking to a bag of bones?"

"Who cares about that now? I'm calling you as a woman and as a mother."

"Okay, I just googled you. You're horrible! You're not even a woman."

"Three million years later and I'm still not 'enough.' For your information, I am a female Australopithecus. And moreover, I'm your mother, give me some respect."

"I might be your descendant, but I'm not you."

"Don't let my appearance fool you, darling, I'm no primate. You are talking to the Mother of Mankind: what came from me *ascended*. I am the vertex of the biggest change the earth has seen."

"Wait. I think my daughter is crying."

"Let her cry. Babies need to cry."

"Now you sound like MyMother."

"You and I are the same, two mothers crossing Time, that's all. Except you're one of many and I was the first."

"The first is still one of many. For your information, nobody remembers you today. I'm afraid Eve's story has sold more copies than yours."

"That's because hers turned out to be more commercial, but it isn't better than mine. In any case, I am the first mother—I don't care if she wins for being the first woman."

"A mother who doesn't even remember how many children she had."

"The key here isn't how many I bore, but what I did with them. They found me next to their remains. Twelve individuals living together. In other words: one of the first families, three million years ago. What I'm trying to explain is that you are the talking to the first mother to have children instead of pups."

"And what's the difference?"

"The difference is that I didn't devote myself to eating apples in a garden planted by someone else. I was the first female to imagine her child, the first to create a mental space in which to raise them, and the first whose children held her hand to walk."

"Why you?"

"There's no one reason. The fact that I was one of the first female bipeds was critical, that's obvious. But there was something else—a leap of faith. Or better said, a leap of imagination. Because, from wherever you stand, someone had to dare to imagine before they hunted. And that's the step that would change everything. It changed things to such a degree that one afternoon, in the middle of the journey back, a female offered her hand to her offspring for the first time, because she understood that they'd make it farther that way."

"Let me guess. That was you."

"Not just me. I'm sure you have also closed a soft fist around your baby's hand. And you've counted her fingers and placed your palm against hers a million times. Do you know why you do it?"

"I'm sure *you* do."

"You do it because that little hand contains our humanity."

"You invented the child?"

"The child and the father, to be exact. Before me, the males just spread semen, let's not fool ourselves. But I changed all that for you."

"I'm afraid things haven't changed as much as you think."

"Ingrate."

"I'm being honest."

"Don't you realize? You are talking with the first woman for whom a man returned home! The first woman to wait for her male in a cave. I am the inventor of the very window you're looking out of."

"Do you think I like looking through this damn window? I wasn't born to wait around."

"Didn't you say you're a writer?"

"What does that have to do with anything?"

"Without motherhood there is no writing and no story to tell. The first mother had to invent memory. And from that woman, the first human being was born."

"Humankind is made up of females in caves and males out hunting?"

"That is exactly what changed our story: the hunters learned to come back because we taught them to remember. Without that kind of memory, there is no child, and without a child there is no return. And if they don't return, there's no food. On top of that, we were able to pursue prey over long periods of time, because man had a weapon that no other adversary possessed: our memory. We were weaker in every other sense, but the trait that turned us into humans also made us stronger."

"Look, I earn my own money, I always have. I don't need some orangutan to take care of me. As far as I'm concerned, every Ulysses the world over can save himself the trip."

"You don't get it, not at all," Lucy whispers on the other end of the line. I think she's about to hang up, which is fine by me at this point. Nevertheless, she continues. "But it's not your fault, it's money that confuses things. This isn't about whether you buy what you need online, or if you use sex to barter with the man who brings you his kill from the hunt. And it's not about whether you're the one who goes hunting, either. None of that matters now. What's important in this story is that we mothers invented memory. And without memory, we would still be animals."

"And what makes you think you taught him? Maybe the male decided to go back himself and you were just some sexually disposable monkey."

"Now you're spewing the worst of the misogynistic

arguments. But yes, researchers are still debating that theory. That's why I called you, to clear up any doubts. Get this into your head: the mother came first. And you should believe me, since *I am the first*. The mother invented the child. Then came the father and, lastly, she taught her companions and her children to remember."

"And then how to give the cave a good scrubbing. I know this story."

"The cave is a space we inhabit in the imagination. What did you think? Our place of return couldn't have been geographic, that would have been of little use to a nomadic family like mine. A mental space had to be conquered. And I did it. That mental space is why you keep watch over your window, not because you think that's where your food will come from. That mental space is why you write."

"The guardian of humankind."

"Our species wasn't the strongest, but we were the only ones capable of following a mental trail. This made our males the best hunters. Because he who remembers always wins."

"Sure."

"Without a mother to save our lives, we'd be a bunch of sorry dinosaurs."

"Okay."

"Park your attitude so you can try to understand. Because there *is* a creator in this story: the female. And an actor: the male. They didn't write the first story, even if they ended up with all the pens."

"Women are still writing stories. Want me to tell you mine?"

"I don't think we have time. You're about to hang up on me."

"Thanks for calling anyway."

"You're welcome. I really enjoyed talking with you. You remind me of myself before I died."

D1 is still asleep with her hands closed in little fists over her chest, like a tiny boxer. The sun is about to reach her eyes, so I gently close the canopy on the bassinet. I open her hands a little and place my index finger in her right palm. Immediately, she squeezes—with strength and instinct. I had never thought about the first female to hold a hand in hers. But I do know, because they taught us in school, that with her clumsy hands that first woman learned to chip rocks into the arrowheads her companions would use to hunt. And only now, as D1's hand grasps mine, do I understand that my hands were made for tenderness. Only now do I know that I touch her with all the love there is in the world. An amount so immense it can only fit in a mother's hands—hands which, today, are mine.

What they told me was all wrong. It was tenderness that forged the first arrow from stone.

EIGHTEEN

First-Person Plural

I was in a café earlier today, writing. Luckily, D1 was fast asleep in her stroller when we got there, protected by the plastic bubble of her rain canopy and encased in a bunting bag. It crossed my mind a few times that I should at least pull the plastic off the stroller and take off her coat: the café was much too warm. But I decided to do nothing and let her sweat, let her sleep and give myself the chance to do some work of my own. Her forehead was dripping sweat.

Halfway into a chapter, a woman came in. She also had a baby in a stroller. This woman did remove the plastic cover and unzip the baby's bunting bag. And it's not like they were even there very long.

"Hello, Carmen," the waiter said, looking tenderly at the baby. "And how is the world's sweetest little girl today?"

"We've been a little impossible, actually," her mother answered. "It's been the same thing all afternoon: we want potato chips."

"Ohhh, does the prettiest little girl in the world want some potato chips?"

" 'Tatoes, 'tatoes, 'tatoes. We want 'tatoes," the woman went on. "We've been crying about potato chips all afternoon. So here we are, even though now we won't eat our dinner."

As I listened, I realized it's not unusual for mothers to speak in the first-person plural when referring to the choral creature we comprise together with our children. Especially when the child does something naughty or annoying to adults. *Whoops, we've peed our pants. We want water. Oh, we fell down. We're being a real pain today, aren't we? It's time for us to get some sleep.* When the child does something good, then the credit is all hers: *Gosh, isn't she just the sweetest thing.*

"Well, here are your 'tatoes," said the efficient waiter, crinkly bag in hand.

'Tatoes, the whole afternoon for some potato chips. The whole afternoon. Her chubby legs in tights, the teether covered in slippery drool. Carmen is a ball of love, a little ball of time. A lot of time, a lot of afternoons.

I have never heard a father speak about his children in the first-person plural. I think about it now, with Man's body close to mine, his arms around me and D1, who has fallen asleep again in the baby carrier. Man alternately kisses my lips and the top of D1's head.

"We like your kisses," I say.

Could speaking in the first-person plural be a kind of madness? How many people can this grammatical category contain?

Rarely does a father end up possessed by his children, while such a state is so common for mothers that it's almost a given. I'm possessed by D1 right now, though I would never admit such a thing to anyone. Yet, in the very depths of my soul, I believe that there are just two people in the room: Man, and us.

Possession is another form of apprenticeship, after all, and we mothers have centuries of training. We've been possessed by gods and men, impregnated without our consent for centuries, from the Virgin Mary to Giambattista Basile's Sleeping Beauty to the woman most recently possessed a moment ago—perhaps this very moment—

by a violent man who believed he loved her.

But it wouldn't be so easy for gods and men if it weren't for the high-intensity training our children subject us to. They form inside us, invade us completely, fill our body and our soul until reaching the most perfect symbiosis, and once they come into the world, they remain inside us in a way that another human being could never do to the man's body or mind. The girl in *The Exorcist* had to be a girl. The devil could have been anybody.

'Tatoes, 'tatoes, 'tatoes. We want potato chips, the mother in the café said, her voice disguised, high-pitched. Who wanted the chips? The mother? The child? Both of them?

After birth, a baby recognizes its mother's voice, her heartbeat, her smell, her breath. Because after delivery, the baby remains inside the mother. Our children stay inside us forever, as any woman who has carried a child knows. And recently, this fact has been proven scientifically: studies have shown that mother and fetus exchange cells during gestation. Our children's cells escape the uterus and scatter inside our bodies in an unsettling phenomenon scientists have dubbed *fetal microchimerism*, in honor of the chimera, a Greek mythological monster that was part lion, part goat, and part dragon. It's not yet clear exactly what those cells do in the mother's body, but we know they aren't limited to passive circulation. The fetal cells that wind up in the heart, for instance, will form part of the cardiac tissue that later becomes a beating organ. So it makes sense that Carmen asks the waiter for potato chips with her mother's mouth.

But before children spoke through their mothers' mouths, the gods did. Apollo's oracle—the Pythia—was a woman, of course. And when she pronounced her prophecies from the temple in Delphos, she always spoke in the first person, with a deep voice she was never heard to use unless she was possessed. The Pythia was the mouth of Apollo and so, in the midst of her *enthousiasmós* (the divine rapture of the ancient Greeks), she spoke in a voice from the beyond. Nowadays, we mothers speak in high-pitched voices when possessed by our children, so enraptured are we all. "What does the hors-eeee saaay?" we ask, in a shriek we've never before produced. "The horsey says neeeeeeeiiighh!" Enraptured mothers always make long vowels even longer. We discover, suddenly, that we love the sound of a nice, long vowel.

Could it be that being a mother is a way of imagining? The Pythian figure appeared in the Bible and survived long into the Middle Ages, converted by that time into witches—the Lamia, terrifying women who were claimed to commune carnally with the Devil. In all cultures, witches have been—and are, still—wise women. The witch is the woman who discovers the sacred and the magic in all things. Who hasn't said this sentence at least once in their lives: "My mother is a witch." Well, now: this is true in each and every case.

NINETEEN

A Father Is Not

I ask myself what a father is, what he's doing here, what he means in our story. I've just gotten home with D1 in the baby carrier (no elevator, so I always leave the stroller out on the landing) and my laptop under my arm. Man is waiting for us. He's happy we're home.

I have no idea what Man is doing with his life lately. There was once a time when we told each other every-thing, talked amongst and about ourselves. But now that D1 is here, I have to admit that I hardly think about him. Being a mother is a kind of boundless generosity that is often directed at a single object: the child. In other words, it's possible Man feels like he's been conned. And so I hug him and tell him how much I love him the moment I see him. He lets me do it, as if he knows it's what he deserves.

We've barely savored that sweetness, that warmth and protection, when a newly sensed truth descends over us. It echoes in my head: We are not in this together.

"I love you," I say under truth's shadow.

And I have the uncomfortable feeling those three words seal my betrayal. Because something inside me whispers that Man is outside of us, of D1 and I, no matter how hard we try to pretend otherwise.

Right away, I know I'm being unfair. Man is good and he tries his best to be part of this singular collective that is Us. But it's impossible for him. Because there are many things that Man is incapable of doing *like a mother*. Such as, for example, something as simple as hearing D1's cries the way I can. And I don't mean that in the sense of personal perception, but actual inability. Because there are some sounds his man-ear doesn't pick up. No, Man isn't deaf, I don't think, but his sense of hearing hasn't evolved attuned to infants' wails. My woman-ear has.

It's four in the morning when I start elbowing him gently. Less gently, now. Finally, I wake him.

"Don't you hear her?" I ask angrily.

I've heard her five times tonight already and I've gotten up every time. Is it possible he really doesn't hear her? Impossible for me not to, even though I couldn't swear as to whether I hear her cries inside or outside my head. In the middle of the night, I don't know who's crying, the baby or me. I have a hard time distinguishing where she ends and I begin, to be honest.

"I didn't hear her. If I had, I would have gone to check on her instead of waking you up. Why did you wake me? It seems like you like doing it."

Maybe he's right, I think. I shouldn't have woken him up.

"I've gone in five times already," I say.

"I'm really sorry, I didn't hear her."

"Can you please go now?"

Checking on a crying baby can mean up to two hours of pacing and singing until they fall back to sleep.

"Of course. I just didn't hear her earlier. I'm burnt out. Try to rest."

And he kisses me. Man doesn't hear D1 because he's more tired than I am. Or at least that's what I'm made to think he believes.

He didn't hear her, I tell myself. And also: *Oh come on, he didn't hear her?!* I know Man isn't lying, so I contain myself.

Since I became a mother, I don't just hear D1: I hear

babies I don't know, I hear them crying from a distance, regardless of where they are. Every time a dusty market appears in a movie scene (always accompanied by the distant wail of a hungry child), every time I take the regional train, watch the news, or visit a new city, I can hear those cries, previously inaudible to my ear. And I immediately think (whether I'm riding in a tuk-tuk in Bangkok on vacation or in a roundtable meeting at work): *Is that mine?* Or even better: I'm chatting with another mother at an indoor ball pit and one of us hears a sharp cry coming from one of the net-enclosed cages. She asks: *Is that ours?*

Obviously, someone had to spend centuries attending to children's cries so that we could make it to this point as a species. It's critical that the young survive. Bid good-bye to *Homo sapiens*, to the encyclopedia, to Big Data if no one's taking care of the children and the elderly. The whole of evolution is cuddled up in a woman's lap. Still, I'm almost positive Darwin never heard the cries of any of the ten children he had with his wife and first cousin Emma Wedgwood. An entire life studying natural selection and biological evolution, only to condemn his lineage to being inbred. Three of the offspring Darwin sired on his cousin died before they were ten years old. And I'm certain that Emma responded to all their cries with love. The things is, choice isn't always selective. And this despite the fact that Darwin didn't marry out of love, but for logistical reasons. He went so far as to produce a list of pros and cons before he committed to marrying Emma; marrying her would give him children if it were God's will, constant companionship (better than a dog's), someone to take care of the house ... these things were all good for one's health, but a terrible loss of time. Without children, Darwin continues, there is no one to care for you in old age, but you have the freedom to go where you like. Darwin was organizing his possessions, female included, the way one organizes one's lands.

Darwin's way of thinking seems very masculine to me. So literal. He leaves no room for ambiguity, a hint of intuition. This kind of rationality proves itself absolutely incapable of seeing beyond the obvious. Clearly Man is better than Darwin, but he doesn't see—for example—all the things that could happen to D1 right now. Everything that could happen if I don't do, if I don't go, if I'm not there, if I fall asleep, if I don't love D1 every minute, if I don't love her more than my own life, if I'm not always there. Man is very prudent, he's even more vigilant than I am, but his attention is of another sort: more realist, probably more efficient, less intuitive than mine, and obviously less inclined toward guilt. No one has taught him this. Man might not even see how guilty I feel when our daughter is upset.

"Why don't you go check on her?" I say.

This time, we're both lying on the couch. Maybe there's even time to take a little nap. D1 is asleep in her crib. We are two exhausted warriors.

"Check on what?" he asks, incredulous.

"Just to make sure she's okay."

"She's fine. She's not making any noise."

"But you never hear anything anyway."

"Do you hear her?"

"I'm going to go check."

Being possessed by my daughter isn't a bad thing, it's actually a gift. It's a real gift. But it's a gift I don't share with Man. He's always by our side, he thinks about us, works for us, he would do anything for us. But Man *isn't* us. Because believing in God isn't the same as being Saint Theresa. Praxis matters. Experiencing ecstasy matters.

Knowing that sex isn't the same as fucking. And fucking isn't the same as having an orgasm. "I had a very difficult life, because through prayer I understood more of my faults. On the one hand, I was called by God; on the other, I followed the world. All of God's creations gave me joy; they kept me tied to Earth," wrote Teresa of Ávila. That class of ecstasy is maternal ecstasy. And you need to be possessed to understand it, because ecstasy is a mystical experience. Obviously, one can have that experience without being a mother possessed by her child, but motherhood's the only shortcut that I'm aware of. There's no other way for me. In fact, every mother I know feels like a mother after she's experienced all of her child's senses. But only a few women and a few men are able to feel what Saint Theresa did. The ecstasy of motherhood is attained through experience and it's available to all. The ecstasy of knowledge is reached through the imagination and it's reserved for a chosen few, like Theresa.

In Man's case, it appears it will be tough for him to reach paternal ecstasy through the path of experience. He hasn't carried D1 inside, he hasn't nourished her with his blood and his cells. Conversely, Man makes a daily effort to incorporate our daughter into himself since the day I gave birth.

Observe a first-time father from anywhere in the world and you'll see just how little time it takes for them to start nibbling their child. Their bum, foot, hand, belly-button. They bite them with rabid sweetness. And the mother will say: *Careful, not so hard.* Just like I say to Man every night after D1's bath: *You're going to hurt her.* What I'm really saying is: *You're going to hurt us.* Fathers are always nipping the soft flesh of their pups, that's the way it is. You have to let them; otherwise, they might try to devour them later, when they've grown. And this is undoubtedly the worst-case scenario. We all know a father who has preferred to devour his children rather than see them grow up to be different from him. And some kid who wanted to kill his father in order to be allowed to grow up differently.

A mother's situation is different. Mothers, for better or worse, live as possessed beings, naturally and socially. Once our children can finally live outside of us and without our help, we get a visit from the *shoulds*, which show up in time to remind us that we can't let our guard down. That we mothers, good mothers, are obliged to love our children more than our own life until we die.

In a year or two, I'll ask myself that question, in the darkness of our bedroom. Alone, without Man. Do I love D1 more than my life? Definitely more than my life? One day, I will whisper it in D1's ear: *I love you more than my own life*. And another night, several years later, I'll tell D2. Both times, something is left hovering in the air.

But there's no talk of this in our apartment today. There's actually not much to say right now. The only thing that's happening is that we've gotten home and Man is happy to have us close to him. He rejoiced at our arrival and has gone off to finish an article in his office. D1 plays with the rays of light streaming through the window and I'm cooking with my favorite music on in the background. And yet, to my regret, I'm poised to go off like a gun before I've even set the table. Right now, a hasty bullet is heading straight for him.

"Why aren't you helping me?" I ask Man.

I'm standing in his office doorway, still as a statue.

"What do you mean why aren't I helping you? Helping with what?"

"I don't know, with the baby, the house. Everything's a mess," I say, glancing around.

"I went grocery shopping while you wrote, I cleaned the kitchen, I made the bed, and now that I'm done, I'm working. Can't I work?" he pleads.

"But *I* never stop. I've done just as much as you have and I'm still not done. I want to know why *you* get to be done." This isn't a reproach. It's a sincere and furious question, but not a reproach. "How do you do it? How is it that there comes a moment when you get to be done? How is it that you have time for *your things?*"

"I don't know. It's never-ending, it's a ton of work. It's hard for me, too. But right now I thought that I could make some headway."

Just then, I hear D1 whining somewhere in the house, very faintly. She's not really fussing yet, but she's about to start.

"Do you hear her?" I ask him.

"Who?"

"Who do you think?"

Man looks at me and doesn't say it, not yet, even though he will, he's going to say it, I know he's about to. Don't say it, Man. But he also has orders to follow.

"I don't hear anything," he says. "You are an excellent mother," he finishes.

I pick up his words and leave.

What is happening to me? At times I'd even say that I view Man as an enemy. It's very strange. Like the motherhood-devil is clouding my thoughts and even my feelings. I somehow find myself feeling opposed to everything I've learned to think, though I have to say that the very act of thinking has become something fizzy, gaseous. I've gained perspective but lost focus. I don't know what I tell myself when I come across a note for something to add to this book: during the seven hundred years separating Hildegard von Bingen and Jane

Austen female writing was scorned because it required thinking, and thinking interfered with motherhood. Is this for real? Does thinking interfere? Can I think, possessed being that I am? At the moment, I'm convinced I cannot. Motherhood impedes me from thinking with any clarity. Though I'm starting to believe that clarity might actually be a pitfall for thought.

TWENTY

D1 Flies with Black Wings

Man is walking down the street, holding D1 and D2 by the hand. I take their picture, and another, and another. I think about posting one on Instagram. I like taking pictures of them, trapping time. The girls hop along, lifting water with their steps. It's rained, and they're wearing wellies: D1's are screaming yellow and D2's are pink like chewing gum. It's autumn, when the ochre cobblestones of Madrid become an earthy carpet of falling leaves. The city resembles a little village. Man and the girls pretend they're hunting for dragon lairs in the sewers. When one is discovered, they quickly stomp on the middle of the manhole cover. Now the dragon can't get out. They pile stones and anything they can find on top. The street is two hundred yards long and it probably takes us more than twenty minutes to cover it: one must be patient, hunting dragons.

It's one of those rainy days with nothing to do, a day I would have suggested going to the zoo, the movies, shopping, to a gallery, a class, or for a drive in the country. But Man said: *We'll hunt dragons.* And so they do. I follow behind because it's my first time and they teach me the art of the hunt. By the looks of it, they go hunting often. While I'm at work—because I am back at work— though we'll talk about that later.

They have the opening of a drainpipe surrounded, the three of them. They crouch down at the same time, slowly and sinuously. I observe my family with satisfaction.

Right now I feel like everything is exactly as it should be, as I want it to be. Is it possible we're doing something right? But then, without warning, without anyone else noticing, the most terrible thing happens.

D2 is huddled between Man and D1 when immense, black wings emerge from D1's back, soft and thick as a Devil's touch. Wings four or five yards high and more than three feet across spread over her little body and unfold over the bodies of her father and sister until all three are captured in a winged embrace. Unaware that she possesses gigantic wings, D1 keeps playing, as if nothing has happened. No one can see the wings, just me. Those wings are death. And at any moment, they could take silent flight.

I'm not frightened by this image because I know that's all it is: a vision, one of my mirages, a maternal fear. And, besides, it is beautiful.

You have forged a mortal family and now you must know that one day I will come and I will take what's mine, says Death.

I know I should shout something to the effect of *Take me first!* But instead, I pretend. I make believe I've seen nothing.

Go on, because I can't hear you, I'm about to say. But I bite my tongue.

That's the thing, you see: at any moment, an innocent walk can become flooded with new thoughts, new menaces. Life with children grants only one certainty: your days of being unafraid are over.

D1 and D2 simultaneously hold all that is beautiful and all that is terrible. All that is good and all that threatens us. They are absolutely ignorant of this. They just want to hunt dragons. But the question is, who will protect them from the fire? I think of Rilke: *For beauty is nothing but the beginning of terror.* And for a moment I hang on to that line, but the words vanish.

It's Sunday. They're still hunting and it's started to rain again. I don't mention the vision of the wings. I don't interrupt them; I don't want to ruin their fun. They see dragons, after all. Their visions are better than mine.

From the rearguard, I announce, "I'm a witch."

"A good witch or a bad witch? Because if you're bad, you're with the dragons. If you're good, you're with us," Man says.

"Mamá is good," D1 assures him, slightly offended by the question.

" 'Ood, 'ood," D2 seconds.

"Mothers are good witches!" I yell. And thank the girls for their confidence.

I'm going to be good, I tell myself. I'm the only one in this family who sees the black wings. I'm the only one who knows what is happening to us. And that's why I'm also the woman who will teach her daughters about the sacred and the magic in all things. That's why I am a witch, because I am the mother. Man hunts dragons, but I breathe fire.

"Mamá! Come help! We need a good witch! This lair is huge!" D1 shouts into a drain.

I rush to her aid. And I position myself between the two of them, beside their father. And then, powerful, I unfurl my enormous white wings. And, for a moment, I keep us all safe.

TWENTY-ONE

Who Is the Best Mother

At some point after my grandmother's death, I began
chasing after rosy-pink babies, babies dressed in white,
with pink or blue ribbons. I had been one of those babies,
after all. MyMother and my grandmother sewed the pink
satin on my baby dresses. Something made me think
that my daughters should look something like theirs
had. And so I started visiting different parks, because it's
not like you can find all types of mother in the same one.
Every park is a kind of ghetto. Motherhood varies across
neighborhoods, much like the use of ribbons, socks with
pom-poms, denim overalls, and organic cotton does. To
see something different, I had to get out of my own very
modern, left-leaning, and mostly vegan neighborhood.

They are easy to spot, those visible, orderly mothers. If
her baby is a girl, she's dressed in pink. If her baby is a
boy, he's in blue. Their babies' shirts are linen, and until
the infants wear little hand-knit jackets, passed down
from parents and grandparents, under they are four
months old. Everything around them is bright and
white, like the most popular photos on Instagram. Here,
motherhood isn't something primitive, it's social. And
I don't know if this represents a respite or if it's just
another trap, but I absorb it with relief. White, freshly
ironed, is the most peaceful color.

I feel especially proud this particular afternoon, strolling with D1 disguised in her old-fashioned baby costume, as if I were showing off a trophy inside the car-

riage. At some point, the sunlight bothers her and I decide to buy a white linen parasol for eighty-five euros and install it on one side of the baby carriage. The parasol is useless and doesn't protect her eyes from the sun, but opening it gives me the same pleasure as unfolding a Spanish fan on a hot day.

D1 is five months old. The parasol doesn't work, but three women stop by our carriage to congratulate me on "how prettily you've dressed the girl." Maybe I am one of them, after all.

This would have undoubtedly been excellent news, since I've been trying to find a group to play with. I wasn't trying to judge the other mothers, I was just in search of a pack, girlfriends I could meet at the park and share everything with. An urgent situation if you keep in mind that—since D1 was born—the closest mother I'd spoken to was named Lucy and had been dead for three million years.

But this question of belonging is a complicated one, because motherhood is not exempt from ideology. On the contrary, in fact—ideology leads to dogma and dogma to disappointment. A substantial part of maternal love isn't anything but good (or bad) upbringing, depending on how one looks at it.

I sit down on a bench next to a mother I don't know and prepare to nurse D1. The woman has three children—all dressed alike—playing in front of her. I cover up with a silk scarf and confirm that nobody is paying any attention. But just then, a conversation starts up.

"I was raised with bottles and I'm still here," I hear the first woman say to a neighbor. "How long did you breast-feed for?"

It's like she's really saying: *When the hell with this end?*

"I didn't breastfeed my first. And he's strong as an ox," the other voice replies.

Some mothers feel attacked by the way a new culture around child-rearing demands primitive fusion with their offspring. I don't know, maybe after concealing ourselves for so long, fusion with our offspring has become more cultural, less instinctive. Or simply lesser. Instinctively, I remove the damn scarf. I watch how D1 nurses. I believe in the resurrection of the flesh and in eternal life, I say to myself, surrounded by tons of kids who, unlike my daughter, will almost certainly celebrate their first communion. I believe in a burning hot nail to which I can cling, in any ocean that will accept me as one of its droplets.

Is there no good answer? Can't a mother be socially sophisticated and instinctively primitive at the same time? Of course she can, the norms we live by are constructed for us. The only problem with such a very reasonable mother is that she is also, undoubtedly, the very worst kind: a *fucking hippy*, the one who shook things up, a 1970s pot smoker—we all know who she is. She's the woman who tried to have it all by not needing anything. Hippy kids don't wear ribbons and their clothes aren't ironed, but their mothers are social creatures. Utopianly, dramatically social. I love hippy moms. I like them because they know that the child they've borne isn't theirs, that he or she belongs to the world and a little bit to everybody. Even the father. They know that anything could happen, given the fact that we're alive, and this knowledge makes their risk a little more human. The problem is that the hippy moms aren't in the park, just on-screen in the cinema and on TV. And I like them, I do, even though in the end they always fuck up their kids' lives, their own lives, even. *Hey, keep my kid for a while because I can't,* they always say at some point in the film. They abandon the child, and deliver a kind of freedom in that abandonment. But those kids wind up with problems (at least in the movies) and their mothers never come back for them. Besides, utopias are full of rules. And rules lead to dogma and dogma to disappointment.

There isn't really an answer. We mothers are received by contemporary society with open arms and democratically spread wings. And yet, when social norms are imposed on the way we choose to mother, supposedly based on "what's natural," we're in big trouble.

TWENTY-TWO

But Whose Is Bigger?

D1 is already seven months old and I know I want to continue with my *professional career*. This is what I think as I walk, gripping a baby carriage and wishing with all my might that I didn't have to go back to work.

As the time to return to normal life approaches, I get lots of questions about this. The people who know me least are the most worried, primarily about the balance issue, which is apparently of interest to women who don't even know me at all. What people want to know—especially women who aren't necessarily friends (those weak bonds, loosely tied but ready to tighten in an instant)—is how many hours I'll spend at work and how many I'll dedicate to taking care of my daughter. I don't understand the implicit general agreement that going back to work isn't actually another way of taking care of her. It is if you're a man: *Good for you! Working so your child has a nice home, food, a level of economic security!* But I'm her mother. The mothers at the park or daycare who spend more time taking care of their kids than working demonstrate special interest in my situation. They ask me empathetic questions, which I receive like threats. I know what they really want to say to me: *I had children to be with them.* Or: *My kids are more important to me than my work.* I'm not sure whether they want to sink me or make themselves feel better, but I'd say they achieve both.

"How will you manage the work-life balance?"

Lorena, her voice as sweet as poison. She's one of the

park's "heavy users." One winter afternoon, I witnessed her actually sit in her son's Bugaboo to warm the seat for his ride home.

I don't want to be as balanced a mother as you, I want to say. But instead I respond, "We're going to do our best."

I use the first-person plural to refer to D1 and myself.

"Are you going to cut back on your hours?" she continues. She's not interested in my response, what she really wants to do is give me hers. "I went down to half-time and I couldn't be happier, honestly. We have kids to spend time with them, and that's all that matters."

There we go. She got it out.

I'm not worried about a lack of time with my daughter, or it's certainly not what worries me most. I shop in the same grocery store as many women who have left their children on the other side of an ocean, for example, in order to have the ability to feed, clothe, and educate them. At this point, some complaints seem morally and politically questionable. What unnerves me is the kind of time that will intrude on me when I go back. In my job, like all jobs, productivity matters.

Basically, I'm responsible for creating and coordinating teams to produce the most in the minimum amount of time. It has nothing to do with producing the very best possible product in the amount of time required. Time is not qualitative in my work. By contrast, the time one spends raising children must be. And therein lies the problem. Because I know that as soon as I sit down in my black leather chair, turn on my computer, and connect my email to my phone, they'll have a watch up my ass before I can even enter my password.

"It's not the quantity, but the quality of the time that counts," Lorena adds. She could stand there spinning phrase after phrase for the entire afternoon, for an entire lifetime. She rests her hand on my shoulder.

Don't you dare touch me, I'm about to say, but I respond smoothly and with resignation.

"You're right, I'll try to at least have quality time with her. There are the weekends, holidays, school vacations—my workday is relatively flexible ..."

She stares at me, interrogating every word, and I know what she's thinking: *This is about clocking hours, every day. Mothers punch in. And at work, your boss is keeping an eye on your commitment to the company. You have to be the last one to leave, even if you're just keeping your seat warm. Our job as mothers is just like any other: we must pursue success, not glory. Besides, this is the only company in which we women have the most stock. Don't you feel empowered?*

Time at paid work is toxic, nobody has any idea how to balance it with the lengthy stamina required by child-rearing, because nobody (not even Lorena) has ever managed to do it. It doesn't matter if you're a freelancer, home worker, actress, engineer, or CEO, because you are the first in this new age. My sneakers don't fit in footprints left by MyMother or my grandmother. The soles on my Converses squash the marks left by their high heels like the tread of some amorphous and brutal beast.

So you won't take unpaid leave, then? You won't cut back even an hour? How often will you get to see her? What time will you get home? Will you be able to keep breastfeeding?

Despite the subject sparking so much interest, no one ever asks me about my salary, or my actual job or field. But the worst is that when in the company of Motherhood, Inc., everything sparkles with the shine of vocation and desire. We mothers resolve to balance the ideal job with a perfect home life. Personally, if I have to die by hanging, I only ask that the noose not be woven of my own expectations.

"Go back to working just like before and pay for the help you need," MyMother says. She's worked her whole life as a housewife.

"But then I won't be able to keep breastfeeding. And the first two years are the most important. It's when the child's personality is formed."

"Just two years? What luck, you're almost done," she jokes.

"Don't make fun of me."

"Take care of your daughter and keep your job. That's what you should do."

"I only want to do what's best for her, mamá. And you know I'd also like to write. It's all I've ever wanted, remember? I don't think there's a writer in history who worked in advertising."

"You know something?" MyMother asks tenderly. "Whatever you do, you're going to end up asking yourself what you did wrong."

"Do you ask yourself that? Would you have wanted to do something else?"

"I'm seventy-eight years old. You can't even imagine how many other things I'd have preferred. I think about it over and over, as if I could erase this or that."

"Did I really turn out so bad?"

"On the contrary, you're perfect. But a mother will always find a way to disappoint herself."

"You did everything right," I tell her.

And we look at each other in misty silence.

"What I want is for you to remember me when, someday, you think that you've messed up with her. I want you to understand me. And for us to be together in this."

"Can't you stop thinking about yourself? I'm asking you to help me not make mistakes *now*."

"I've already told you what you don't want to hear. I

promise that breastfeeding for a month or two less is not one of the things you'll think about when she grows up."

Six months after going back to work, D1 no longer nurses and I am what they called a real *working mother*. I have a new social status that is admired and pitied in equal measure, depending on the forum. Curiously, the label *working father* doesn't exist, nor does a particular feeling run through a man who both works and raises his children. My feeling—the feeling of being a *working mother*—is as real and unmistakable as a brick wall. A labyrinth of brick walls. For instance, I feel a dangerous inability to distinguish between what is urgent and what is important with respect to almost everything. Wall. I live in an ungovernable mental mess that, when it gets to be too much, I try to deal with by tidying the living room or kitchen. Wall. I have doubts about pretty much everything except the certainty that I'm living on the edge of a huge mistake. Wall. The path of yellow tiles my shiny red shoes once walked is now littered with pebbles and unnecessary fatigue. Yet, even if it's the most circular path possible, I do believe it's also the one that will take me the furthest. I don't know for sure; something else I have doubts about. Wall. To feel safer, I make lists, which serve no purpose other than making me believe that I'm doing all I can. Wall. I've even added already-completed tasks at the end of my notebook if only for the inexplicable pleasure of crossing something off my checklist. *Buy rye bread, shoes, theater tickets, hang the baby's smock up to dry, read the frog book.* Well done, everything under control.

Cross off, cross off, cross off. Doubt, doubt, doubt. Wall, wall, wall.

TWENTY-THREE

The Sea or A Wall Painted Blue

I'm caught in a traffic jam, an eighteen-month-old daughter at home and another in my belly, snug under the special seatbelt for pregnant women that cradles my stomach as I drive to work in the ninth month, packaged in an SUV with leather interior and an Isofixed carseat in the back.

Surrounding me on the highway are hundreds of cars with one person wasting time in each. There are many of us stuck drivers, those of us trying to keep our jobs, those of us with mortgages, who don't make love as often as we'd like, who wish it would rain, or simply want to make it to next summer. I've never seen anyone get out of his or her car. The cars only stop in the event of a serious accident. Many are headed someplace they don't want to go, but only death or fate will get them out of it. And so here we are, spinning golden thread out of our days.

Since becoming a mother, going to work has become little more than a way to force myself out of the house, to not be where I should. Work is like a cage, but it gives me the freedom to come and go from home as I choose. Because there is always a cage. And maybe paid work is my way to have, on occasion, the keys to my own.

Nevertheless, sometimes reality peels away like adhesive backing on a sticker and then, my car idling in traffic, I see a part of myself turning the key and shutting off the engine. I imagine getting calmly out of the car and sitting down on the asphalt, without bothering to turn on the hazard lights. The other drivers are getting angry, they're waiting for me to take out the reflective orange safety triangle from the trunk and indicate a problem. But my horizon is cloudless, all is calm here inside myself. I could be staring at the Mediterranean sea or a serene blue wall, all that matters is that I stay calm and wait, eat up time. I'm not sure what I imagine will happen, or why I'm even taking this little mental trip, but before I can uncover my reasons, the car in front of me moves forward a few meters and I drive on in the direction of traffic.

I don't think it's my fault. I know I don't lack love or determination, but I still don't know how to do better. Nor have I found anybody who definitely does, a clear example to follow. Maybe we humans only know how to live like this, glued to both our clocks and our desire. Maybe this is why I go to the office every morning. Afraid, hungover, lazy, sex still on my lips, swallowing my sorrow. It doesn't matter if you're a laborer, artist, or physician; you have an automaton inside you who bolts wherever it thinks Death isn't waiting, like in the fable. I love that story.

Once upon a time, a wealthy and powerful Persian strolled through his garden accompanied by one of his servants. Said servant was downcast because he had just come across Death, who had threatened him, and so he begged his master to give him his fastest horse so he could flee and reach Tehran that very evening. The master obliged and the servant galloped away.

Back home, the master also came across Death and asked, "Why did you threaten and terrorize my servant?"

"I didn't threaten him," Death replied. "I only expressed my surprise at seeing him here, since according to my plans I had expected to meet him tonight in Tehran."

There has always been Death, but there was a time—many, many years ago—when there were no clocks. And at one point, money didn't exist. But then the world changed forever and there is not a human being alive today who can go off the clock, anywhere in the world. There is a clock in the medieval square of a repopulated ecovillage, it's just like Big Ben, with the same numbers as the Spasskaya Tower and a second hand like the Makkah Royal's. Clocks are everywhere, from kilometer zero in the Puerta del Sol to the golden gears rising over Fifth Avenue in New York, Hong Kong, or Piazza San Marco.

Death and money, the things clocks measure.

We all adhere to invented time, injecting worry into our bodies. Money made this worry inevitable. And paid work takes care of measuring it. In this light, the equation is a logical one: bigger worry, bigger salary. Later, we will all flee in traffic, terrified as the servant who fled to Tehran. Motherhood is another unknown in that same equation. The mother who worries the most will be the one who receives the most love.

I ask myself which one of these traps is worse and all I can do is scream that I'm much more than a sack of time as I follow the silver ass of the car ahead. I could say, for example, that I am love for my daughters, that I am food for a human soul. But I don't, I don't say it because one small detail ruins it all. Love should beat like a heart, not tick like the second hand of a clock.

There has to be another way, I'm sure of it. A parallel universe right before my nose, as real as the fairies who live in forests. Unfortunately, a very thin veil over my eyes keeps me from seeing the obvious. Still, that's no reason to stop looking.

Over the past few months, I've done some collaborations in a coworking space for creative types, some of them freelance, lots of artists and craftspeople, a few writers. Nothing serious, of course, our bills are too punctual for me to be thinking about making a real change, but I've dropped in on their enormous, dilapidated studios from time to time, just in case.

Right inside the main door, there are two large racks full of pajamas, accompanied by two large, instructional signs: *I don't work alone.* And: *Almost all the pajamas are unisex.* Unlike my current company (which has never shown any concern for what I sleep in or any other personal affairs), this freelancer cooperative is trying to create a more supportive and less aggressive workplace. Concretely, there are eighty-five people working under the same roof and basically sharing fixed expenses (space, electricity, WiFi, kitchen, printer, phone ...), although the ultimate goal is to also share experiences that provide some kind of value (market value, I suspect) to the others.

Two Fridays a month, they organize speed meetings, which consist of personally meeting everyone who works in the same coworking space. Or anyone who they consider merits being introduced. I'm invited to one of them, I expect because they suspect I have some kind of commercial value. My acquaintances here know that I work at the agency, after all, and the agency means the marketplace. I like to investigate other ways of organizing my life because I'm sure there are better ways to do things somewhere out there. I only need a superficial glance to know these coworkers don't have the solution for me, but I'm consoled by the knowledge that they're trying.

The problem with the sociology of work is that you blow all graphs and charts to pieces when you add the motherhood variable. The average worker must resist being alienated by work, but a working mother is already alienated by her child.

The working mother is the best possible employee, because she's the one who will take anything. I know that if I was a business owner, I'd do everything in my power to hire as many working mothers as possible. We are the perfect employees, the ones with the most to lose.

A mother has to choose. Think, or work. And if she doesn't work, she doesn't feed her kids. The holes dug by bills can only be filled with money and we good mothers know that income starts with the letter W. Work. And work means dedicating our time to someone it doesn't belong to, in exchange for money we need to make everything else possible. Would I have more time if I became a freelancer? Could I live better with less? More equations using the same unknowns.

For the speed meeting, we form two big lines facing each other. I get to be part of the group that doesn't move, so I just have to sit down. People in the other line will take turns sitting in the chair opposite me for seven minutes. A little over an hour to consummate ten professional encounters.

A man in his early thirties is sitting across from me. D1 is with me, snug in the baby carrier. I've finally stopped using that archaic piece of fabric I never quite got the hang of and switched to an organic, ergonomic backpack.

"We had a baby six months ago," he says, looking at either D1 or the brand of baby carrier, I'm not sure which. "It's absolutely crazy, but it is possible to have a balance. We share the childcare fifty-fifty so we can both continue our freelance work."

"How can you guys make any decisions if no one has a majority?" I ask.

"Wait, what do you mean?" He raises his eyebrows slightly.

"I mean, it could also be a forty-sixty situation, or fifty-one and forty-nine. Equality taken to the extreme might complicate some of the decisions you have to make about the baby. You'll be living in an eternal technical tie in the event of discrepancy."

The thirty-something laughs. He's wearing a black Motörhead T-shirt.

Our seven minutes are up. I think D1 is hungry. I should nurse her during the next round. I wonder if the fifty-percent father-mother I just met uses a nipple shield.

Until recently, we women were the ones invading the men's world, and naturally, now the men are demanding their fifty-percent share of child-rearing.

I've also come to terms with spending less time with my daughter in order to occupy a space in the labor market. I feel good about another woman bringing her to the park while I'm earning money that will pay, among other things, for the woman that brings her to the park. I feel good, too, about her father bringing her to the park while I work so that they can enjoy that time together. I like earning my own money, as I've said. But I don't believe in fifty-fifty responsibility in child-rearing as a general concept. Or at least I hope we won't be so stupid as to concede fifty percent of our domestic power to men before we've managed to gain fifty percent of economic and political power (assuming those are even different these days). That would be so typical of us.

Of course, there are specific cases in which everything is possible (there are fathers raising kids fifty, one hundred percent of the time ...). If we bring up specific cases, the possible universes multiply. But when we speak "in general," we have to acknowledge the median statistics and not the outliers. In general, mothers still have less economic and political power than men and shoulder much more of the burden in the domestic sphere.

That's why I don't like when a man talks to me "mother to mother," just because he's wearing a baby carrier. Typical men. They change their reality and conclude they've changed the world.

Poor kid. He seemed sweet. Maybe I'll listen to some Motörhead today.

TWENTY-FOUR

The Time to Act Has Passed

D1 is putting toys in a box. Next, she will joyfully dump them out. Then put them in again. I know I should pay attention as she does this. If I'm not attentive, she could fall, stick her fingers in a socket, choke, bump her head. Just a few months ago, I sometimes felt like she was stealing my space, as I debated whether to devote myself to thinking or raising her. But that choice no longer exists: I have literally stopped thinking. It's no longer about having a room of one's own inside or outside of the family, because there isn't enough room for it all inside of me.

My awareness of the world has expanded to such an overwhelming degree that I feel closer to all the souls on Earth. And much further away from my own.

I wonder when it will happen, the first time I don't want to occupy my time with her. The first time that, when presented with a choice between life and daughter, I choose life, the other life, the life that was mine alone and nobody else's. I suspect that the demands on my attention won't let up for a second until Time and Love close the first door. And I know that will be a long time coming, because now D2 is on her way.

I bathe D1, dry her off, kiss her, play with her, mix a scoop of baby cereal with seven scoops of formula, add 240 milliliters of water and shake, shake, shake at night, shake, shake, shake in the morning, the same hand and the same container: the bottle free of BPA, a harmful carcinogen found in plastics that we well-informed mothers, the best mothers, carefully avoid. Then, I put the frying pan on the back burner, to avoid burns, add olive oil (one night, two nights, three hundred and sixty nights) and I fry, bread, sauté ... While I hand Man a glass of wine and do the grocery shopping online from my laptop on the counter.

How long do we have to pave the way? As I walk my own narrow path, I celebrate the brambles other women have cleared for me, but it's still a path plagued with briars. I wonder who the hell I'll find when I finally cut through the brush and make it to the castle and I sure hope it isn't a sleeping woman that a man will kiss without her permission. I don't want to kiss her myself, either. Whatever our destination, I hope to find a woman who is awake. Or I'll have to kill her with my own two hands.

In any case, I'm not too concerned about this at the moment. I feel increasingly comfortable in my role as a mother. I've been raising a little girl who is now two years old and I'm about to give her a sister. For the first time in my life, I am what I want to be, for the first time, love and duty dovetail perfectly. It's been a long road, but apparently what I have right now is something we might call a *real life*.

This feeling has been spreading inside me like a stain. When I got pregnant with D1, I had nine months to assimilate what was happening to me: I went from being a pitiful mortal to a divine being. Gaia, Mother Earth herself. That's when I started to feel bad for men, who are incapable of giving birth. Something inside me will always pity them, mere mortal accessories to me, mother and only necessary being.

The miracle of creating life inside one's own body is such a commonplace and overdone topic that it's hardly been considered in a social or political light. But deep down, we all recognize the unparalleled power it implies. I'm thinking of poor Zeus, stomping his feet like a child over his masculine failure. Not even the gods could cross that line reserved for the magical bodies of women. Such was young Zeus's desperation that he consumed a pregnant Metis so that their daughter, Athena, could be born from his body, from his virile head, in fact. But Zeus was a god and his whims weren't appropriate for mortal men, and perhaps this is why they have spent all this time fighting each other for what is earthly and fleeting, like money and power. Sad compensation for those who have been condemned to a life without transcendence, for those who can't sew life to death. That invisible thread has been women's exclusive domain for millions of years.

Since becoming a mother, I've thought more than once about how, to some degree, we've accepted our social inferiority in exchange for a different kind of elevation. While my body was creating a heart and pancreas and two lungs and a brain and nose and two beautiful eyes, I became convinced that anyone who couldn't be a mother was in fact an inferior creature. And from that day on, I felt that I really had nothing to prove, that any social success or achievement falls far below the shine of eternity with which women polish human existence. That magic is female in origin. And it is, perhaps, the only thing worth living for. It was difficult to hold up my feminist principles after becoming a mother, to be honest. Deep down, a part of me believed for the first time in the superiority of one of the sexes.

But things are changing quickly. Zeus's dream is ever closer for men, because today the mother's body is more expendable than ever before. We can implant another woman's egg in order to have our child. But we can also put another woman's egg inside ourselves to have a baby for her. We can even put in another woman's egg with another man's sperm in order to give birth to a child who won't have a mother at all, but two marvelous dads. Today, women can be mothers or they can be Zeus's head (and we can be paid a lot, a little, or nothing for this service). And we can be Zeus's head freely or under coercion or exploitation but, in one way or another, parentage is no longer what it was. It has changed forever. By previous agreement and under contract, a mother can give up her right to be mother of a child that she will give birth to, a child who will not have the right of being the child of the mother who bore them, at least not in every case.

Of course, this is happening at a time of an unrivaled and definitive global movement for women's freedom. There is precedent, of course, but this movement is different in the sense that—for the first time—we've had everything taken from us, even the one thing that was solely ours. The least we can do is demand equality.

Beyond that, the fact is that when life is subjected to scientific efficiency, science will name a price and procreation will become another form of power. Fine, Margaret Atwood predicted it first. We could talk about the genocide of the feminine and we wouldn't be wrong. But towards the end of my first pregnancy, my belly tight and perfect as a mermaid's tail, I didn't care about anything other than my protruding belly button.

Later, after D1 was born, in the midst of exhaustion, confusion, and life, I knew one thing for sure the whole time: I wanted to have another baby. And when my first daughter turned twenty months, I was already pregnant with D2. We were so sure we wouldn't be able to have children without more in vitro that we implanted both of the frozen embryos we had left. We had to use them before we could start another round of ovary stimulation, the doctor told us. Having another child was going to mean another lengthy financial nightmare.

The genetic quality of our embryos was so poor that it hardly made sense to implant them, but the law prohibits the destruction of all frozen genetic material, regardless of its quality (once in the uterus, it can be eliminated). So we paid about a thousand euros for them to inseminate me with something like "embryonic waste."

Still, D2 furiously clung to life and the scientists considered it a statistical deviation. But it wasn't. Sometimes scientists forget the most important thing: that life doesn't gestate in mathematical medians but in its dispersion. And that each individual is a particular, unique case, the opposite of any model.

So that's how we got here. To this body that is one with D1 and joyfully awaiting D2's arrival. Incidentally, I think it's important to highlight that there's been a change that might ruin my story: I am no longer Mother Goddess but Mother Conduit, the woman providing the transport for new goddesses. A simple, necessary woman, never to be divine again. This is the difference between creating life and raising children.

Even so, I know that I'm something other than what I was before, before I started to devote my love and time to other beings, before my bringing them into this world. And I know that I'm not necessarily a better person because of it. It's not just that I form part of something bigger than myself—I *am* this bigger thing. A drop of water in the ocean can be a drop or it can be the ocean. And light and heat enter through the windows and I see specks of dust floating in the air, little specks I hadn't noticed since I was a child. Happiness is a state of innocence.

The only thing disturbing my contented state of good hope are the voices of all those women chit-chatting in my kitchen. What the hell are they doing here? Lately, they've been coming every night. And books, clearly, are to blame. Because those women wouldn't have anything to say if I hadn't read them.

"Fifteen years from now, girlie, you'll be just like me, you'll have messed it all up." Grace Paley speaking, with unruly hair and knowing smile.

"Get out of my house right now," I reply.

"Perhaps the meaning of a woman's life consists in being discovered like this, seen in such a way that she herself feels radiant," explains Carmen Laforet.

"That is exactly how I feel now, Carmen dear," I say. "So we're not going to have this conversation. I know exactly where you're going with this."

"What a writer needs is a pencil and a piece of paper." Ursula K. Le Guin takes a turn, jabbing at my throat.

"I don't feel like writing right now," I assure her.

"You end up comparing your life not to the one you would have wanted, but to those of other women. Never to that of a man," Annie Ernaux pronounces.

"Disappear!" I spit in her face.

Ha. Ha. Ha. They laugh as they leave. And I hear myself pleading, " Leave me alone."

But voices keep coming through the door. Or through my head, who knows. "I lacked self-esteem," I hear one say now. It's MyMother's voice. What on earth is she doing here? "If I could have known ..." My grandmother. "I had to raise other women's children," my great-grandmother replies. Dear women in my family, I'm not going to listen to you. Your stories will never be mine.

I know what you've come to tell me, but you're wasting your time. I don't need anything more. Can't you see the way that Man is looking at me right now? Mine is a true love story.

Man watches me from the woods, from the window, from the passenger seat, from the pillow, from the beach, from the terrace. I am the mother of his children. How hard is it for you all to understand that I don't want to be anything else? That no love is as perfect as our love, that only we have been able to give D1 life, that against all odds we've cleared the way for D2?

I want you to understand once and for all that I have everything a woman could desire. And you are forbidden from annotating that sentence.

Now, get out. All of you.

TWENTY-FIVE

Witch in Velvet

D1 is dressed up as Cinderella . She's wearing a blue tulle dress with gold glitter and she's put on a pair of miniature silver high heels that someone must have passed down to us. She can buckle the thin straps by herself and stand up on her "heels," which is what she calls the sparkling shoes. "So This Is Love"—the song from the Disney classic—is playing on Spotify. My daughter spins down the hallway with outstretched arms, the dozen golden butterflies sown on her dress fluttering over her chest. The royal ball is to be held in the living room and I'm waiting for her there, because I'm the prince. I watch her come out of her room and am captivated by her innocence. She looks me in the eye and makes a small curtsey, blushing slightly. We dance and fall in love over the course of three or four minutes, but then the alarm on my phone goes off. The bell tone: TAN-TAN-TAN-TAN-TAN-TAN-TAN-TAN. D1 looks at me, dripping with love, and takes her leave with a bat of her eyelashes. She runs down the hall, sure to leave a shoe behind, halfway between the ball and her wicked stepmother's mansion. Before I can catch her, she reaches her bunk bed—the room where she lives with her wicked stepmother and stepsisters. There, she will be my servant and I will speak to her in the cruelest voice she can imagine.

I quickly take off my pajamas and slip on the black velvet dress whose train, at one time, trailed across a thickly carpeted floor. The dress has a high neck and a completely open back. I'm seven months pregnant and have gained almost forty pounds, almost entirely in my belly and breasts. I'm not wearing a bra because everything is in its place, taut, ready to burst. At the moment, nothing needs to be held up, and the black velvet lies on my breasts like a premonition. I've thrown my hair up in a messy bun and I'm tarted up so clumsily that when my daughter sees me, she hangs her head and asks:

"Do you need me, stepmudder?"

"CINDERELLAAAAAAA! Have you seen this mess?" I complain in my most wicked stepmother voice. "You must clean it up, all of it. Sweep, mop, cook, wash all the clothes from the ball. It was horrible. The prince spent the whole night with some brat. No one knew who she was."

"Now, prince," D1 demands.

I turn my back and, in the middle of the hall, take off the dress and put my pajamas back on. I pick up the shoe and knock on her bedroom door.

"Does a girl live here?" I ask, holding out the silver shoe on a pillow.

I greet the two stepsisters, a giant stuffed bear and a Nenuco dolly, and check that my daughter is hidden on the top bunk. The shoe is too small for the bear, and too big for the doll. Impossible to make it fit. Undoubtedly, neither one is the girl I fell in love with the other night. A third girl appears at last, descending the spiral staircase (or bunk ladder). And now ... now it's Cinderella's turn: the shoe fits like a glove. We give each other a kiss and run off to celebrate in the living room, where we spin and spin until we collapse on the couch. I'm exhausted.

"Again, mamá! Again!"

I look at her, spent, and smile. The last time, I promise myself. She goes to her room and everything starts over.

"CINDERELLAAAAAAA!" I shout from the living room.

"Yes, stepmudder?" she replies with happy obedience.

Man is reading in the corner of the room and lifts his head now and again to watch us come and go. Now he will be the prince, I warn him, because it's what D1 prefers and because I want to focus on my role as villain.

Much later, as D1 sleeps, we lie in bed after falling asleep on the couch and sleepwalking to our room. Man says, "I want you to wear that dress for me."

"What time is it?" I whisper, half asleep.

"You're my stepmother, now," Man says. "I'll wait for you in the living room."

And though I just want to sleep, I obey. Because I know that, for a busy mother, sex is the only thing that can drive away death. I'm not talking about making love, you don't need a costume for that. I'm talking about breaking down the walls of a family so that we can feel like we still have the chance to be who we want. I'm talking about a return to furious, frantic sex, sex to stop time, to escape, to dissolve freely in another body and revel in that mortal victory—orgasm.

But the truth is that I'm half asleep and I'm not really sure that I can be roused. It is often a challenge to jump the boundaries drawn by love and to simply fuck. Raising children can confuse a couple, turn lovers into mere relatives: two become one, but in service of the child. And one can't fuck properly without confronting two realities, two shadows that, against all odds, add up to light.

For Man and I, with one daughter in common and with another on the way, there's too much tenderness between us, an excessive domestic complicity.

In other words, after bathing her, very carefully drying her hair (given her low tolerance for untangling snarls), feeding her (having removed the tiny fish bones from every morsel), brushing her teeth, wiping her bum, reading a story (and one more), tucking her in, and then going back to her room (turn on the light, read another story, smooth on lotion, cover up a stuffed animal that's gotten cold) … after doing all of this between the two of us, practically unaware of who starts a job and who finishes it, and with my belly bursting with another baby, it's a challenge to find a man inside Man capable of wanting me with the passion another woman would inspire. Man loves me from inside my very being and that mixes everything up. At some point, it might even ruin it all. But not today. Because tonight he has demanded that my flesh fill his body with silence once more.

I rise without a word and get a stepladder from the kitchen to take the box of dress-up clothes down from the attic, where I put away the stepmother's dress after we played. I undress, my body as chilled as my naked feet on the tile floor, and I put on the wicked, backless black dress. Then I walk to the living room, the velvet train dragging across the floor like the dirtiest of desires.

And there is Man: naked, separate, a stranger, sitting on a couch that doesn't even look like ours, a statue prince who has lost his girl after too many dances.

Man slides his hands down the back of the dress to make sure I'm not wearing underwear. He directs me then, with stray words. Tonight, he only speaks the bare necessities.

Kneel.

Get up.

Turn around.

The doors to the balcony are wide open when I feel Man's mouth on my back. I rest my elbows on the coffee table so I'll have something to lean against when I take him in, and look out at the night, black and thirsty. He lifts my dress and there's the brush of fabric on my skin until I feel his hands touch my shoulders, and grip them. There was a time when sex with Man served to make us one, to consummate something close to wholeness. But now that he is my family, what I need is for him to give me back my borders, to make me separate from everything inside myself that is not me. Everything inside myself that is him, even.

I don't say anything. I won't even look at him. I'll barely touch him tonight. I just have to wait and give him room. My enormous belly is hidden from him in this position, and his hands find my swollen breasts.

I feel his eyes lock on the back of my neck and in our silence I can hear that there are two of us, that I don't know what Man is thinking. And so, when his touch becomes that of a stranger, I open the doors to my darkness and ask Man to come inside. Man must accept that he will never know everything about me and he will never be everything to me, and in spite of this, he just wants to howl together, to release all the darkness that threatens to harm us. And so he grips me until it happens, we're both wolves, pain and pleasure are one and the same and we're finally alive again.

I don't say anything when he's done. I get up, let the dress fall, and go out to the balcony to take in all that is new. Then, I go back to bed. And sleep, at last.

TWENTY-SIX

Welcome, D2

I think about how two people who have loved the children they share can stop loving each other. How they can split up, separate, hate, come to detest one another. How do they come out of this magic? How could Man stop being the best of all men after he's sat beside me with D1 in his arms, after tying the horrible robe they make us wear when giving birth in the hospital, after looking at me like there was nothing else in the world? I don't think anybody can take away our memories, except ourselves, that is. Because I don't know who we'll be when she gets here, the same way I don't know how the hell you can need something when you already have it all. We were the perfect couple, the three of us. But we wanted more. I wanted more. I'm scared of wanting more, always more.

I was afraid of D2 before she arrived, afraid of what she could do to us. I had a hard time believing I had enough love for so many people. I thought that, in the event of a shortfall, Man would end up the loser: no milk for you, no bed for you, no home for you, no life for you. And I felt awful about the thought of something like that happening to us. And I felt awful for D2 though I hadn't even met her yet. Failure is always possible, a good geneticist would say. What if D2 were to ruin our lives? Who knew what could happen? I'm not convinced that having a sibling is automatically for the best. Go ask Abel if he liked having someone to play with.

D2 puts us all in danger, I thought. I was scared. Scared of myself, and above all of what I would do if I didn't have enough love, which I felt sure I would lack when she arrived: I had all the love in the world, it's true, but I had already split it between Man and D1. By my logic, it followed that very soon there would be a deficit for one of my daughters, for him ... Back then, I still wasn't thinking about whether anything would be left over for myself.

Some nights, D2's little kicks echo in my body like the beating of war drums. Like tonight, when I'm five months pregnant and having dinner with Rosa Montero, the writer. I'm wearing a loose camisole over skinny jeans.

"I'm pregnant," I tell her, stretching my top over my early baby bump.

"Again?!"

No one else says this. People say *Congratulations, that's fantastic, how far along?* But Rosa, who is my friend, says *Again?!*

"Yes," I reply.

She scrunches her face. I know what she's thinking.

A lot of women write with kids, and they do it with a lot more than two. Nobody thinks you can deliver something more important than a baby. Except Rosa. Rosa has been my friend for a long time. The first person to read something I wrote. And against all odds, to keep insisting that I don't abandon it, despite everything else. Including this belly, which to her alone isn't sacred.

"It will be two more years of full-on baby. But then I'm going to find time, you'll see."

She doesn't really buy into the whole thing about my expanding consciousness, etc. She isn't one of the dead women writers in my kitchen. She is here.

"Did you do it on purpose?" she asks, and orders

another bottle of white wine to wash down the news. "You can drink wine, right? Have a glass at least, or a sip. We need to celebrate!"

TWENTY-SEVEN

You Were Conceived Mortal

D2 was born with a soft, wrinkled mouth, pink as an omen. I had never seen anything so beautiful.

Her throat concealed a switch that she used to shut out the rest of the world so I only heard her hunger and urgency. From the very first day, D2 was magic. Maybe that's why I wasn't very surprised when I discovered that she had brought along two little packages when she came into the world, leaving them for me to find among the sheets on her hospital bassinet: one imaginary parcel with extra love for D1, and another for Man.

"Thank you," I said. "I think we're going to need them."

D2 came from a far-off place, from the land of You Will Want For Nothing, and I was firm about taking us to live there. I would bring my family to live, safe and sound, in a place where they would want for nothing that I was able to give them.

How many more times could I do this? How much love do I really contain? How much more can I deliver? I ask myself from my hospital bed. D2 is just a few hours old and I'm watching her on the white sheets.

We've been given a bouquet of pale pink rose buds and I've placed them beside her, arranged in the white light of the hospital. I amuse myself with comparing the color of the flowers to her lips. I watch as she opens her hands for the first time. I watch as everything happens for the first time. And bit by bit, very slowly, the color of the light entering through the window changes. That light, the caress of time over the flowers. D2's first light.

We're alone when the doctor comes to see if we are ready to be released, to go home to celebrate. She does not release us. I don't know what this doctor is saying. I think she's saying that something doesn't work, something faraway out there, far from us. And so I look at D2 to confirm that she's still the prettiest baby in the world and that anything else is impossible. But the white coat won't stop talking, won't pay attention, the white coat keeps saying what she's come to say.

"It isn't necessarily serious. I don't think it's affecting her brain," she says.

She lies. Because if the word *brain* crops up in the sentence, it's serious.

"But what's wrong with her?" I ask.

D2 is in the crib, far from the words *brain* and *serious*, asleep.

"We believe she suffers from craniosynostosis," she explains.

This clarifies nothing for me.

"I don't know what craniosynostosis means, doctor."

"It means that some of the bones in her skull have closed prematurely."

"Prematurely, in my womb, you mean? She formed incorrectly in my womb?"

"It means her skull has closed early. The bones of the cranium shouldn't be sutured at birth. When this occurs, the baby's head will be shaped abnormally and it could affect the brain's growth."

"But her head is completely normal," I say.

"It looks normal, yes. But if we confirm that the cranial sutures have formed, then those little bones could become a cage for her brain, which still needs to grow. And for her head. That's why it's important to act to correct it quickly."

"How do we correct it?"

"For now, we need to wait two or three months and see how she develops. We can't be one hundred percent sure that she has it, or that her brain is affected."

There they are again, the percentages.

"Does that mean that it's possible there's nothing wrong with her?"

"The neurosurgeon will come by to see you this morning to explain the next steps. For now, you should rest," the doctor concludes.

She leaves and D2 wakes up. She starts to fuss. I don't think she wants to hear her mother crying alone. She wails louder and louder, and so do I. It is a moment of complete loneliness. No one else knows what's happening. They think everything is fine, when nothing is.

"Welcome, D2, life greets you in all its splendor," I say.

Man and MyMother are downstairs in the cafeteria, ready to come get me and take me home with all the flowers that will fit in the trunk, with the layette and stuffed animals we've bought for the girls—a blue hippo for D2 and a polar bear for D1. All the softness of a receiving blanket. But none of that is going to happen now.

D2 has pooped. Newborn feces is thick and black as tar and has a special name: meconium. The doctors are pleased when the meconium is out of the baby's system and the intestines start working normally with extra-uterine food because this means everything is okay. I learned this already with D1. This time, the diaper soaked with that nasty stuff made up of dead cells and stomach and liver secretions, I know there is no way back. I thought I'd brought an angel to Earth, but it isn't so; I absorb this realization over the filthy diaper. And I confess a secret to D2 that I have never, ever told D1.

"D2, my child, you were conceived mortal."

I hadn't planned to tell her for years, five or six at least. But D2, only a few hours old, is already a woman.

It's hard to explain what happened next. But beneath my white postpartum slippers, a huge hole split the sanitized tile floor in two. I think I passed out. As if knocked unconscious by a blow to the head. Pain put me out. I abandoned D2. I gave up. And I awoke much later, or much farther away, in the warm hospital bed with a pillow on either side. And there was D2, intact in her transparent bassinet.

The neurosurgeon who comes to see me is actually a very young woman.

"The baby is too young for us to diagnose craniosynostosis. We won't be sure for some time," she explains moments after entering the room.

Redheaded, tall, kind, and freckled, she still has the air of a mischievous child. Not now, of course, now she's as serious and plainspoken as her professional certainty, or as a dismissal.

"When can they confirm it?" I ask.

"In four to six weeks. But I want her to have an ultrasound before you go home."

"An ultrasound of her brain?"

"Yes, to rule out any other abnormalities."

"Other abnormalities? But we're not even one hundred percent sure of the first one."

"We're not. But in cases like this, it's better to prevent if we can."

"What is our case, exactly?"

"Craniosynostosis can only be corrected if detected in the first weeks of life. If we confirm your daughter has it—which we still don't know—we will likely have to operate. Early diagnosis is critical for proper development. That's why we follow any suspected cases very closely."

"But is it a problem with her skull or could something be wrong with her brain?"

"I think we will all be comfortable after an ultrasound."

"What would the operation consist of?"

"It's a relatively simple procedure. Minimally invasive, which decreases the risk of hemorrhage and facilitates recovery. We have to go into the baby's skull and open the sutures that have closed prematurely. Nowadays, the only risk is blood loss during the operation. But typically, patients only require three or four days in the ICU."

"Do you believe my daughter has craniosynostosis? Is it a clear case or is it possible there's nothing wrong?"

I look at D2 and place the words *risk* and *hemorrhage* on her pillow. It can't be.

"Again, we don't know. But you can feel that the little bones in her skull are closed when they shouldn't be, just by touching her head. Look." She takes my hand and places it on D2's little head so that I can feel for myself. "Obviously, we can't diagnose by touch. We think she may have it, but that doesn't mean she definitely does."

I let her leave and I go back to sleep, quite possibly even before the door closes behind her. I sleep for a long, or possibly very short, time. Man and MyMother are still in the cafeteria, so it's possible this winter has only lasted a couple of hours. Meanwhile, they still think everything is fine, that we're about to pack up to go. They're probably eating one of those hospital sandwiches with chunky butter. And a beer. What the hell? Maybe even a glass of white wine. Maybe they've toasted in celebration.

I've done nothing to stop it, of course, because that's exactly how things should have gone. But it's obvious now that they can't continue. I have to call Man. I ask him to come up alone, to tell MyMother to wait a little longer in the cafeteria. All this time, which actually hasn't been very long at all.

"We need to take the long view," Man says. And he squeezes my hand. And looks at me. "We're lucky to be in a good hospital, with the best doctors, in the best hands. In the event that she does have it, which we don't know, we will be lucky to have detected it in time. D2 has been born in a place where, fortunately, everything can turn out just fine."

Then MyMother arrives.

She pools on the floor like a puddle of water. I can't go to her aid, I can't even look at her. Impossible to mop up the pieces of MyMother from the tiles. I leave her there, undone. And before I fall asleep, I speak to her as coldly as the doctors spoke to me. Worse, I speak to her as coldly as a daughter can speak to her mother when her mother needs her.

"We have to wait now, mamá. You should go home and get some rest."

Nothing is colder than my voice.

TWENTY-EIGHT

Mental Analysis

I'm seated on one of the plastic chairs in the neonatal ICU, waiting for them to do the ultrasound on D2's brain. I see babies on breathing machines, babies full of needles, purple babies, babies twisting in pain. I see their mothers' faces watching the incubators through a pane of glass. Little creatures that can't be touched, that their mothers can only hold for the amount of time strictly regulated by the ICU. I grab D2's hand. She breathes on her own, digests on her own, pees on her own, poops on her own. She doesn't need help to survive.

A couple sits down next to me as I wait. They're dressed in street clothes, they smell of city. I, in contrast, have worn the same nightgown for three days. This means that they've had to leave without their baby.

A doctor appears before us. I don't look up, so I only see his clogs and the bottom of his white coat. He doesn't want to talk to me. He's looking for them. So I keep my head down.

"I have bad news," he begins naturally. It's obvious this man has spoken those same four words many times in this very hallway. For him, tragedy is nothing new; it's only tragedy. The parents tense up next to me, like two cats at an unexpected noise. The doctor continues, "Though we were optimistic yesterday, things have gotten worse overnight. As soon as you went home, he started to turn purple. We don't know why, his lungs are seriously affected."

"But he's never had trouble breathing on his own," the mother says.

As if there had to be some mistake. Bad news is worse when it's unexpected.

"Until yesterday. We had to give him oxygen to keep him alive. And his lungs filled with fluid."

"How could something like this happen?" the father asks in shock. "We left him sleeping peacefully."

"We don't know. But he also has a collapsed intestine. He vomited everything he ate. His weight is back down, but that's the least of our concerns. We reinserted the feeding tube, but this caused problems with his kidneys."

"But we gave him his first bottle yesterday. He didn't need the tube the whole day."

"His heart has suffered, as well," the doctor continues. "We've had to revive him twice. Last night was extremely complicated."

"But he's okay now?" A thin voice asks, the sound of glass just before it breaks.

"The situation is very serious. There have been failures in his respiratory, renal, and gastrointestinal systems. You should prepare for the worst," the grave voice responds from inside the white coat. Firm. There should be room for compassion in firmness.

This doctor doesn't speak in probabilities. Despite being a doctor, he affirms: *You should prepare for the worst.*

Because there is something worse than everything he has already told them.

I was alone when this episode took place, and even today I doubt that it really happened. The doctor's clinical account seemed a cruel joke, a lie. I felt like laughing. Had I imagined this impossible scene as some sort of macabre comfort?

Suddenly, the white coat vanishes, the other parents disappear. A doctor's voice calls D2's name and both our surnames to go in for the ultrasound. Unexpectedly, I don't give a shit about the results. I'm not afraid of the word *brain*. I'm not afraid of any word.

Because as they're finishing up D2's ultrasound, I know that she and I are going home this very afternoon. I know that D2 can survive on her own and I know that, right now, this fact is more important than any brain. It's actually the only thing. I feel even happier than when they give me D1 to bring home, no shadow hanging over us. There are things about my daughters I still can't know. Maybe that's why I will never live another day without fear. But for today at least, I know that her body is sufficient enough for her survival. And I understand that this is all I can hope for. My youngest daughter has come to teach me.

A doctor stands beside the ultrasound technician and explains that her brain is fine, but that we need to repeat the ultrasound in a few months. Evidence in a baby only two days old is insufficient. But at this time, they don't see any damage. We'll come back in eight weeks.

TWENTY-NINE

Where Is the Love

D2 is already nine months old and it's been too long since anyone brought me flowers. Maybe that's why I've started writing, jotting the first notes of what will become this book. Every spring, MyMother used to pick roses for me. Until I left home, I always had wild roses on my desk. Dark-petaled roses, almost purple. D2 was born in April, when roses bloom. There will be more in the future, just not right now, because now isn't the time for flowers.

Craniosynostosis was definitively ruled out eight weeks after we were released from the hospital. Strangely, the time we had to wait wasn't filled with anxiety, despite the fact that I usually can't help looking up every symptom online. But it wasn't like that with her. That's why I believe D2 frightens away uncertainty. She is all sureness, the opposite of melancholy. My opposite.

I could have spent the eight weeks in anguish, I could have thought about all the bad things that might happen, I could have talked to Man, or MyMother, about how afraid I was, I could have told someone about the operation and the blood and the hemorrhage. But I restricted myself to being her mother.

Then, with our two daughters safe at home, the time came for us to lay all our cards on the table. The time came to face the most perfect love that has ever been.

At some point I realized that I had the ability, the power, to make my daughters happy. And I was also aware that my love for Man was so complete that it could produce daughters. Not just any daughters, but our daughters, undoubtedly the very best creatures on the face of the earth. And we had to learn to live with all that. We would slowly have to get used to the fact that some things turn out right. And some times, lots of times, everything turns out right at the same time. We were all alive. And we all loved each other. And I'm not talking about just any love, but the most irresistible kind of love, one of the best things that can ever happen to you. Like when D1 pulled a needlefish from the sea with her toy fishing rod, or when they fell asleep in their princess costumes, holding hands. Or the afternoon we destroyed the sandcastle we made together, D1's bare feet, D2's mouth full of sand. Why do babies always want to eat dirt? The first time D1 drew something and demanded we recognize what it was. The first image was a papá: a straight line in the middle of a white page. Then a mamá. A parallel line, thicker and longer than the first one. Then she drew herself: another line—thicker and longer than the other two put together. All three in blue. And below, her sister, much finer, much smaller, but close to her line. Choosing a new favorite color, chocolate-covered popcorn stuck in the couch cushions, the darkness on the night we went out with our red flashlight in search of wolves. And the stars, and D2's first word. Not *mamá* or *papá. No,* she said. The sound of kisses blown in the air, her arm hanging through the bars of her crib (she could get hurt), an afternoon spent picking cherries. The fruit's red flesh and her mouth stained with that sweet, wild juice. The first scare, the first swing, a brown mare with a white mark in the middle of its forehead and its foal suckling beneath, the Three Wise Men. The best things that can happen to a woman. Better than that, every woman's dream: to be the mother of her daughters. To be everything, Mary Magdalene, the Virgin Mary and the manger, all of it and all at the same time. That, and to have enough money to buy all the ideas I've been sold. Don't forget anything on the shopping list:

- Romantic love. Two rations in the cart (value pack)
- Man of my dreams (save receipt)
- Mortgage (requires an empty trunk to pick up)
- Two jobs (one to live and another to be alive)
- Anti-cellulite shock treatment (Flash Effect)
- Two babies (one grown and the other not quite done)
- Baby seat with built-in anti-tip security
- European election system
- A brand-new cape (mine must be red)

These past few years, I've felt like a superwoman. But we know that kryptonite can take down Superman, and I have always been the equal of my male counterparts. I clearly had to confront my own weakness. I'd be a shitty superhero if I didn't, after all.

Love, I'd already intuited, is the source of my female vulnerability. There's a lot of propaganda about love, a lot of noise, songs, too many interested parties.

Love is draining and sometimes it's depleted out of sheer exhaustion. Love is oil, the real black gold. A natural resource that keeps the wheels turning. And we mothers are something like the OPEC of love. We can fit a lot of poverty into our slums, we know how hard extraction can be, we know there are limits, that it won't last a lifetime if it isn't managed well. This is why mothers the world over repeat the same sentence to our children every night: *Turn off the lights!*

It's taken me more than four years of child-rearing to understand something as simple as the fact that love can't conquer all, not even the very best love in the world, not even ours. In the early days, when things weren't going quite the way I wanted them to with Man, I believed it was because there were too many imperfections, that we had to prove our feelings time and time again. But I had nothing to fear, because when Love isn't enough, Sacrifice is waiting in the next room ... She had been sitting there a long time, watching me as I shopped and crossed the items off my list. And she wasn't waiting just for me. Sacrifice is always waiting, for all women.

I have more clarity now. I can see beyond the white cotton curtain that separates one room from another. And I know that, someday, I'll have to shred that veil. Because the day will come when the girls will cry, complain, get sick, bite, shout, break a plate, kick, throw up, spit, or raise their voices and I will have to pull back that curtain. Sacrifice will be on the other side, she'll greet me politely before coming in. And that will be just the beginning. Because I've been programmed by the many women who came before me to sacrifice for my daughters until it hurts, until love succumbs to routine, until I'm repeating the same thing over and over, until I'm bored. I'm designed to surrender to emptiness, because this is what it means to be a mother, one who "does it all for her children." Ready to love my daughters and my man even when they don't deserve it, because that will be "when they need it most." Let's not forget that words serve as commands and I have been served words ever since I was born. And so on, until one night I'll end up telling two teenagers flopped on the couch (their legs spread too wide): "Someday you'll understand all I have done for you."

Of course, now that I know this, I could go on with my life in a different way. Pay them less mind, start to accept what they will become. But in order to do that, I'd have to drive a stake through my heart while shaking D2's bottle with my other hand. There is a *should* inside me, a *should* that's not even mine. And that *should* says loud and clear: *Give up writing, give up going out at night, give up reading for now, give up work, give up everything that isn't them, because everything will be where you left it when the little girls you see before you have turned into selfish tweens who only need you as something to hate. And you know what? The reason they will hate you is because you didn't give everything up for them. You insisted on living and you will pay for it.*

And so at this point in the story, I cover my ears and close my eyes and shout. Because I don't want to be interrogated or answer any questions or think too much about any of the women my girls might someday become. Presently, I'm the only woman in the house—and even Superwoman can't predict the future.

D1 is three and D2 is twelve months and I know one thing with absolute certainty: I am the happiest I will ever be. Because:

1. The girls are fine.
2. Man is fine.
3. We're all fine.

THIRTY

Obey

Being a mother is the way women train for submission in the modern day. We have broken away from some injustices, and we're still in the struggle to topple others. But when it comes to motherhood, love collides with a set of expectations that we didn't devise but which we take great pains to fulfill, consciously or unconsciously. We become creatures ripe for domestication. Music calms wild beasts and motherhood pacifies women.

Although I have always considered myself an expert at rejecting what didn't suit or belong or agree with me, I find that I have learned to comply with orders unquestioningly. To give in, to smile, to make peace at the party. All for their well-being, of course. But also for my own sense of doing things right. D1 speaks fluently now and she uses her all her linguistic determination to achieve her will. She tries with everybody, but her success rate is much higher with me than with any other person. For her part, D2 has learned to say four words with which she can obtain everything she wants: *papá, mamá, yes, no.* I'll admit I've come to find intimate pleasure in doing exactly what they ask of me, in making them happy with anything that won't hurt them.

It would be difficult to list all the demands and commands I receive from my daughters every day. I think I've stopped registering them. After much practice, I've learned to obey without thinking or talking back.

MA-MÁÁÁÁ! I WANT. Come. I'm hungry. My __ hurts.

Play with me. I'm hot. Carrot. NO. I want to watch a movie. My belly hurts. The princess shoe got broken. I need tape. Scissors. Cut this. NO. The bunny's lost. Read me a story. Turn on the iPad. Turn off the light. MA-MÁÁÁÁ! I DON'T WANT TO. Give me a kiss. Don't tell papá. I want watermelon. YES. Get my undies. I peed my pants. I have to poop. I want to go to my friend's house. Can we dance? I don't want to wear that. Those tights bother me. Put my mermaid tail on me. That skirt is ugly. I'm not going to have breakfast. MA-MÁÁÁÁ! NO, NO, NO. Brush my hair. Will you buy me something? I want chorizo. Not like that. It hurts my ears. Brush my teeth. Tickle me. I want a bubble bath. Popcorn.

I expect we humans obey—because of the systems we live in, or how we've been raised—at least one out of five times that we are asked to do something. Once we've been trained, one out of three. As a mother, I manage to obey every single time something is asked of me; it's much more efficient than arguing. The problem is, once you learn to do it, once you can obey with a smile, once you can count to ten for the second time, once you know how to control yourself, once you understand that it's best to be patient, once you have learned to keep your mouth shut—you become anybody's mark.

Luckily, today is one of those days that no one has asked anything of me yet. It's two in the afternoon and we're still in our pajamas. The house smells like food and warm saucepans and Man is waiting for me in the kitchen with a cold glass of wine and freshly steamed shellfish.

Right now, Man's hand is under my chin. A nibble on the lip. The hardness of the counter at my back. The girls are playing in their room. Our bed is still unmade. Lunch will have to wait. The perfect family.

"I have to pee," I say. Man's weight presses on my bladder.

I like when he squeezes.

I've had to pee for at least three hours but I haven't found the time. I've been holding it. I've become an expert at holding it. All I have to do is think four magic words: *And then I'll go.* I'll make the bed *and then I'll go*, I'll get her breakfast ready *and then I'll go*, I'll break up their fight *and then I'll go*, I'll shower *and then I'll go*, I'll run out to the grocery store *and then I'll go*, I'll put on some music *and then I'll go* ...

"Go pee," Man whispers in my ear.

"We'll fuck *and then I'll go*," I reply.

Ten or fifteen minutes later we're done and I finally burst, maximum pleasure. I really needed to go to the bathroom.

It happens when I wipe myself. A sight that fills my head with a thousand words, an image that slices right through me. There is a light, but unmistakably brown, stain on the toilet paper. Poop, even though I only peed. But the evidence is there on the cotton, a judgment on me and my body. I am dirty. How could something like this happen to me? How the hell did it happen? I guess I must have gotten up from the toilet earlier before I finished wiping, rushing to attend to some domestic emergency, such as turning up the volume on the cartoons, and never went back. I imagine Man discovering it during sex. It could have easily happened. Maybe it did! I just went to bed with him like this! I imagine Man licking my ass and finding himself face to face with my filth. What am I doing with my life? Why am I waiting to pee for hours? Why don't I have time to wipe my ass? I get right in the shower.

The hot water scalds my butt cheeks and I'm ready to collapse. I'm sad for myself. I sit on the floor of the shower and let the water flow. I feel like I'm living with some unacceptable person, and the problem is that I don't have the faintest idea what to do about it. And this makes me furious, with myself and with him. I'm furious with Man because I suspect that somehow this is his fault.

But Man hasn't realized that this is not going to be a good day for us, he doesn't know we're going to fight yet. We're going to fight unless he comes in here right now and explains to me why, of the two of us, I have to be the dirtiest. But he's not going to do that, because this is one of those times that Man has no idea what I'm going through.

I get out of the shower and dry off. I choose my best body lotion. I put on perfume and skin cream. I want to be clean for the rest of my life. I smooth on the lotion with circular strokes and kick off a logic-filled soliloquy. I tell myself that I should demand Man take on fifty percent of the responsibility for everything, that he help me more, that he obey the girls as much as I do. I apply a bit of conditioner and brush out my hair. We'll separate our bank accounts. That could be the other key. I will monitor that Man does exactly the same amount of housework as I do, that we both bring home the same money (or I'll put on record that I make more). The goal isn't to divide the visible work evenly, or even the money. Man visibly works as much as I do, both in- and outside the home. The real problem is something else and the solution will have to be, too. The real problem goes beyond sharing roles, even the ones you don't see; some roles are more of a burden, they weigh more than others, no matter how often he carries the heaviest suitcase at the airport. What I need is to share the mental space of child-rearing, all the domestic thoughts I think for the benefit of the four of us, the invisible and uncountable effort Man benefits from. For example, starting today, I want Man to make lists of everything we have to do, make note of all the things the girls will need as the season changes, read all the WhatsApp messages from the parents' group at daycare, know whether or not we have lights for the Christmas tree, know the name of the cortisone-free lotion D1 needs when she gets dermatitis, research how the fuck to sew the carnival costume for school because he feels it ought to be homemade and he should sew it himself, be on top of all the unimportant things that somebody has to think of, get off the toilet with shit on his ass and go turn up the TV so they won't start crying. I want him to never stop. That's what is needed to fix things. That is the key to this issue. I don't want him to ever—I mean *ever*—have time to sit on the couch as if nothing is going on. I could kill him when I see how freely he uses his spare time, guilt-free, worry-free, as if the girls weren't even there.

In just a minute, this very day, he'll go to the living room, sit down, and pick out a movie we both might like. Before it's over, he'll fall asleep and take a long siesta. And the worst part is that he doesn't even know this is going to happen. He doesn't even need to plan, because he can still do whatever he feels like in his home; being a father hasn't changed that for him. On the other hand, I'm already thinking about what to feed the girls, because they don't like seafood and I'm not sure last night's fillets are going to cut it. We have green beans in the fridge, but I don't have the strength for that battle. And to top it off, it's already gotten really late for D2, who hasn't had her nap and has clearly missed her mealtime. And precisely because it's gotten so late, I won't be able to get her down after lunch, and if she doesn't rest, neither will I. But I really do need to close my eyes even if it's just for a goddamn half hour. Only that's not going to be possible because when she cries, Man will be satiated and relaxed and I will be the one to get up. I might fall asleep, too, but even if that were the case, my sleep would be lighter than his. That also pisses me off and I feel entirely justified, even when the cause for my anger hasn't happened yet. Because it *will* happen, exactly like I say. Because I'll drink less wine at lunch, I'll be waiting to hear her cry, and I'll go to her as soon as I hear it. Then I'll soothe her with all the tenderness in the world and feel the smooth violence of everything that isn't working like it should. This is why I'm adamant that we need to share the mental space. I urgently need to feel that my head is as free as his. That, and a better place to live. We obviously need a better place to live. Now that I think about it, it would make a huge difference. Does he not see that, either? Doesn't he ever think about this family?

"I think we should move," I say, raising my glass to Man.

I've decided not to bring up the subject of mental space. We'll start with this other one.

"You're scary when you start thinking like a real estate agent."

"We've been in the same apartment for ten years and ... I don't know, I'm not sure this is the right place for us. And, by the way, I'm sick of thinking about things that affect all of us but only seem to be a worry for me."

"Try to remember that housing anxiety would make nomads of us. And that this itch you get is always a symptom of something else."

"Do you realize that every time I express a different opinion, you accuse me of being anxious or hysterical or whatever else will discredit me?"

I told you we were going to fight.

"I realize that every time you want to move, we have an argument."

"Well, I just think that we could set ourselves up somewhere nice, I don't know. Have a terrace for the girls, a bit more space. Something better, you know?"

"I don't know. The girls love this apartment, because we've been happy here. But you think we'd be happier with an elevator, despite the fact that we have no problem going up and down stairs ... Help me understand what you think you need in order to have it all."

"Maybe you're the one who 'has it all' already, because I feel like I need something else. An easier schedule, for example? More time for myself?"

Man doesn't get that when I demand more exterior space, what I actually need is to feel like I have ownership over my interiority. But that's something I won't confess, not even to myself. It's really hard to say what's wrong without it seeming like it's my fault, like it could all be different if I would just behave differently. Maybe in a penthouse, you know, or in one of those corner ground-floor apartments with extra yard space in a development outside the city. One of those houses you buy off-plan. Some confirmation that things are going as they should be despite the fact that I have shit stuck to my ass.

Only now it's too late. I suppose I should have started sharing the responsibilities and tasks the day D1 was born, like the kid in the Motörhead shirt at the coworking place. Still, I know who my girls will call for every time they have a nightmare. Something inside of me doesn't quite believe in fifty percent.

Yes, it's definitely too late. Maybe I should have stopped working altogether in order to avoid this situation. Maybe our modern way of organizing ourselves works less well than when the woman was financially dependent on the man, but at least had time to be home with her children. Given the fact that I seem to be holding the worst cards anyway, maybe it's not such a bad idea to hold fewer than he does.

Up until the 1970s, there were few women in Spain who didn't have the primary goal of devoting themselves to a family. In addition, the vast majority gave up work when they got married or had their first child. Women were insufficiently educated, very few advanced their studies, and the majority got married. Back then, getting married had a purpose, and a good husband (rich, cultured, powerful) could be as valuable as a good job is nowadays, because it assured women material support and the time to raise her children, at the least.

Since 1979, the number of female students enrolled at the Complutense University of Madrid has exceeded the number of males. Today, the norm is inverted: many of us study and fewer and fewer of us marry. The sociologist Luis Garrido wrote an impressive book on the subject: *Las dos biografías de la mujer en España* (The Double Biography of Women in Spain), in which he sums the case up more or less like this: in 1980, 65% of Spanish women between the ages of 20–34 were married; in 2016, the figure was 19%. The institution of marriage is no longer useful (it no longer protects either of its members in any special way) and is therefore in danger of extinction. Garrido calculates that, if current trends continue, in 2030 there will be no married women between 20 and 34 in Spain. All the while, the birthrate also plummets.

And so Spanish women (Western women, in general) study more, work more, marry less, and have fewer babies. And what happens when we decide to study, work, pair up (or get married), and to top it all off, have babies? Well, what happens is that we ruin our lives. Because we play with marked cards, and good intentions won't ever be enough: the house always wins.

Childhood and old age are the two stages of unavoidable human dependency. But the State has decided to only finance old age and couldn't care less about our children. Working mothers (and their children) are, in some respects, even more disadvantaged than other mothers before us. More educated, perhaps, but more disappointed. Because just when we can have it all, we bear the curse of not really being able to have anything.

"Haven't you noticed that I'm like a chicken with my head cut off, that something isn't working how it should?" I ask Man, serious and full of reason.

"You are not a chicken. You are a strong, intelligent woman with your head on straight."

"I'm more and more convinced that there's no way to be a good mother, a good professional, and a good partner. It's impossible, we all know it's impossible. But some of us choose to fail in the attempt rather than accept the obvious."

I am relieved. Telling the truth has always been a source of relief for me.

"You scare me sometimes."

Traditionally, men have not learned to feel the need to nullify themselves in order to raise their children. On the contrary, they've been concentrating on other issues for millions of years. I don't need to cite any studies on the subject because everyone knows it. This has been their ancestral advantage and today it continues to be the reason why men are still found at the top of any ranking or statistic related to power or money. It's not that the world has been made to measure for men, but rather that men invented the ways of measuring the world.

And so now, as hard as I try to split the work fifty-fifty with Man, I know it's going to be hard (impossible, really) to share this invisible space with him, the space occupied with the care, surrender, and worry of the mother that I am. And as long as I feel alone in this place, some arguments will be unavoidable.

Sometimes I think that we will only have a fighting chance as a species if men are able to recover and reclaim their own femininity. I don't think this is asking too much, given that women have jumped through all the hoops of their capricious masculinity. Which woman hasn't had to show someone that she's worth just as much as a man?

Book I of Kings (3, 16–28) describes the method Salomon, King of Israel, used to discover the truth in a judicial case brought before him: a dispute between two women, the son of one having died. Both claimed to be the mother of the living child, more or less.

One woman says, "My son is the one who lives and yours is the one who has died." The other says, "No, your son is dead and mine is alive."

The King says, "Bring me a sword."

The King was brought a sword, and without further ado: "Cut the living child in two and give one half to each woman."

Then the woman whose child it was spoke to the King (because her guts twisted for her son) and said, "Oh! My lord! Give her the boy alive, do not kill him."

"If I can't have him, no one will. Cut him in half," said the other.

And the king replied, pointing to the first woman to speak, "Give the boy to that woman, and do not kill him. She is his mother."

I'm my daughters' mother and something inside me (several millions of years inside me) will never accept a Solomonic division. I will wait for D2 to cry after I eat and I will go to calm her and I will be a zombie playing with her on the rug in her bedroom. Meanwhile, Man will sleep. And when Judgment Day comes, I will say that he's the best father in the world, that he deserves them more than me. And I'll tell the presiding judge that I don't want shared custody, that their father can keep the kids so they don't have to leave their home and all it entails. I will explain that he is a wonderful father to his girls. And I'll do it because, secretly, I will never give up my fifty percent, because I love them a little more than anybody else, even their father. And maybe that's why I live in that secret, invisible mental space, the space that might be the end of all of us. The sacred place where many of us women dwell in service to everyone, and which, at the same time, does nobody any good. That space is a political space the State has relinquished. We should be paid to manage and occupy it, independently of whether or not we have other, paid jobs. We should feel that we are objectively recognized and reassured, and as long as this doesn't happen, we are all in danger. Because a society that has pissed off its women is a society in danger of extinction.

The worst part is that when D2 finally cries and I go to get her, exactly as I had predicted, I tenderly observe Man and tell myself that it isn't his fault he fell asleep. I tell myself that I shouldn't get angry over something like that. Then I feel enormous sadness for us both. Such a shame that, having made it to this point, the antidote for all our ills is also our poison.

Die once and for all, romantic love, goddamn romantic love. And give us the chance to love each other in peace. When I return from getting D2 down again, exhausted, arms half asleep, back aching from her weight, I observe Man and his impassive repose again. Then I know that he is guilty, I know that I was right from the start, and I feel, once again, the stain on my ass. My ass, my sadness, but Man is the one who has sown this shit between us. I lean over him and whisper in his ear:

"You should be awake, you fucking bastard."

THIRTY-ONE

Shipwreck of Happiness

I've never felt so happy, so full, so complete, so whole as when I was mother to one- and four-year-old daughters and living with Man, the father of them both. Interestingly, this state of intense happiness turned out to be somewhat intoxicating and decidedly overwhelming, hard to manage.

Happiness is an excessive feeling, impetuous, like the sea when it swallows a chunk of land (house, bar, entire beach) with its enormous, splendid waves. The explosion of nature: beauty and terror, Rilke again, together again. And that's exactly what happened to me. I was mistaken, happiness is not dead calm, it is not lying on your back on a hot pink float in a blue pool. Happiness can destroy everything in its path, rip away what you have and even what you don't while you contemplate the scene, exultant, not knowing whether you're witnessing your own wreckage or your triumph.

I'm in our bed one Sunday morning and I'm so happy that I don't dare move. I want to stay exactly where I am, observing the mess of our room in the weak morning light. And yet it turns out that—without moving a muscle, without a single word—I also want to get out of bed immediately and get the house squeaky clean so our family can spend Sunday in a pleasant, orderly home. I want order, family, predictability, a pension plan. And I also want to leave everything as it is—the dust bunnies under the couch, the tiny toys scattered across the floor and pricking the soles of our feet, the dregs of wine in last night's glasses. I would even enjoy seeing an ashtray full of the cigarettes we smoked back when we used to smoke properly. An ashtray that will never come near my daughters. Can you imagine the smell?

There's nothing I can do: happiness is a weapon loaded with desire. And I've become a woman armed to the teeth, and I hate violence. Me, a bomb, ready to go off. But that's how it is. Happiness can be in two places at once, in two moments, two desires, two feelings. And so, even though I don't want to be separated from my family for an instant, I want to travel the world on my own, carrying nothing but the backpack from my youth. I want our house to be the very best—the very loveliest—of all. But I don't want to have a house, or a car either. Oh! And I want the girls to play in their own backyard. And to get another, bigger car, one we could all sleep inside in the middle of the woods. And I want to go everywhere on a scooter and be a real writer and not have a wallet, just a change purse with no credit cards, nothing but a few clinking coins. And I want to never have to think about money. I want to play. And to work, sometimes. I want someone to pay me for something that I can do better than other people. I'm talking about a job that requires a lot of qualifications, so they pay me for my work, instead of buying my time. I think about taking a long family walk through the Retiro and maybe stopping at the magician that tames a stuffed lion with his Indiana Jones whip. Or going to that restaurant near Algete I heard about, the one with bouncy houses for kids, that could be an option. But, before any of that, I have to get up and I don't know if I'm ready, because it is Sunday, after all. Though, now that I think about it, I had better get writing if I want to make progress on this book. I can't let my family life eclipse my career. It's horrible, it really is, but my family is the enemy of my success. Clearly, success requires time and we all know what a family feeds on.

All of this occurs in the blow of a gale and I still haven't moved from our bed or from our Sunday. But the light is slightly disturbed; maybe I've made too much noise. I look at Man. I love watching him wake up. I tell myself that I must act responsibly, I must organize all of this, make some space on this side of our front door for everything I am. Before a wave washes in and carries it all off.

What I obviously need is a lover.

I have to tell this to Man, here with me on this Sunday morning. "I'm ready to be used for the first time again: there's a new package that needs opening," I should tell him. I've suspected it for a while, but there's no longer any doubt. And I should explain his situation to him, too, because sometimes it takes Man longer to figure things out: "Open all the packages you can, honey, because I know very well what you're going through." But Man is really and truly calm; he's still in that peace that precedes convulsive happiness. He doesn't seem to want more than what we have. He's not spilling over yet, he's not as happy as I am, he doesn't love me as much.

His waves aren't as high as mine.

THIRTY-TWO

The Body Is a Literal Animal

My body is no longer what it was. It used to be a temple of pleasure, now it's a temple of comfort. And Man knows it. Before I was a mother, I had a body to enjoy, to feel, to be, for him. But I'm a love factory now. Now, I really am a female object. I have a chair-body, a bed-body, a hammock-body. I am all of these things, and in the meantime, I slowly disappear.

D2 has just turned one and she uses me to fall asleep, to calm herself, to rock, to cry, to rub her fingertips across my nails when she's afraid. I would have sworn that fingernails couldn't be a comfort and I would have been wrong. My girls have lots of obsessions with my body. D1 pinches my arms when she's sad. When she's missed me, D2 chews on my face. They have colonized my skin and they have broken ground. They've built a gas station, a 24-hour pharmacy, a supermarket, a mall. I am a dispenser of amenities. I keep new secrets in my lace bra: wadded-up tissue, for example. Carrying tissues seems more critical to me than wearing underwear. I'm also handy for sucking. And not just my milk: my thumbs make a great pacifier, my knuckles, too. Even my elbow. In their judgment, all of me is up for grabs, and will continue to be long after I've weaned them.

They're three years apart. According to the World Health Organization, breastfeeding is essential for the first six months, recommended for a year—then comes the farewell weaning and the end of being sucked, as long as they use a pacifier. But soon I'm pregnant with D2 and everything begins again. Since we had the girls, there are lots of things I'd like to ask Man. Do you remember when I used to suck my finger for you? When you were the only one to taste these nipples? When I used to suck you? Can you even imagine? Now that the girls do it too, sucking is something else. And when they've finished devouring me, you and I will both know that this body and these breasts are theirs. But there are other men who won't know that. And I will want to feel new again. More or less how I'm feeling now.

The day I breastfed D2 for the last time, I knew I would never do it again. That my body-mother-food status was coming to an end, that night, in that bed. We die so many times. A mother is also all the bodies that have died inside her.

D2 looks like a freshly landed fish when she nurses, silver slip of a thing. I watch her open and close her mouth with the sweet desperation of hunger just prior to being satiated, a brilliant blue fish out of water that could perish if I don't nourish her. I can see the sea of my childhood while you nurse, D2, from right here in the Plaza de la Paja in the center of Madrid, more than five hundred kilometers from any shore. I swear to you that you will never lack for air. I would let you drink my blood, drop by drop. May you never lack air, my little fish. Eat. Take comfort, for this is my body.

What can Man do with a body like this?

Can I be another woman, separate from this body? I doubt whether I can keep loving Man now that this flesh is other and means so many new things. I think I probably can't, there cannot be continuity of love after this rupture. And Man knows it. He has realized that I'm another body, and therefore another woman, another person. We can't underestimate the body's importance. I have to accept it: Man is sleeping with someone else.

My breasts have two holes through which the cold and the outside world can enter me. I feel them reach me even when I'm wearing a coat, and under that coat a jacket and a shirt and a camisole and a nursing bra, and, inside the nursing bra, round, absorbent pads that keep my milk from seeping through my clothes. But the truth is, I wear these dressings to keep out the cold. I'm not going to stain my shirt; nothing is going to spill. If the baby doesn't suck, my milk doesn't flow. But the fact is that if I don't protect myself, everything external can enter, the outside becomes part of my flesh. A little pinch here and another there and there another. It's the soul of the world sneaking inside of me. It's the way I stare at the shoes on the man holding his child's hand in the market and the pride on his face as he squeezes that small hand, and it's the polish buffed onto those old shoes, shoes that should shine like new when worn by a father who wants to feel proud. It's the first roses in Madrid's Anglona garden, petals wet with rain, and the woman selling fruit, plucking her tomatoes one by one from the box. It's all injected in me with the chill of a needle. The red lips on the twenty-year-old girl with freshly straightened hair at noon.

Now that my body is consolation, I wonder what will be most important to Man, comfort or pleasure. I tell myself that sex itself is, as much as anything, a form of consolation. Vibrators aren't called *consolodores* in Spanish for nothing; they're not called stimulators or arousers or electronic pleasure dispensers. Of course, it's women who use vibrators. Man would prefer porn, prostitutes, or a blow-up doll. Because Man is a man. I think about what men look for when they're willing to do anything to have sex, when they're willing to pay for it. What is a man looking for when he goes out whoring, what will Man look for, my man, between those sheets where a good man never goes, only monstrous strangers, only other men. Do my friends' husbands see prostitutes? Did my father? Do my colleagues at work pay to be serviced?

A woman's body is not the same thing as a mother's body. We can't role-play that I'm your whore anymore, my love.

Have you ever been with a prostitute, Man? Tell me. Have you ever even fantasized about paying a woman to use her body with you? Well, if you've ever paid for a kind of consolation you couldn't get from me, you can save your money now—because from this day forward, you will never find another woman who makes you feel as safe, as secure, as fearless, as the mother of your children. And that's me.

Whether or not they use prostitutes, men are excited by them. They're excited by the idea of being able to pay for relief. I myself would pay a high price for the pleasure of comfort.

It's hard to feel ownership of your body when it's permanently exposed and available, a body that feeds on demand, responds to demand. A body that is the permanent object of desire for the most defenseless creature on Earth: the child, the newborn.

While I'm nursing, I feel as fragile as my supply of milk. Then there's D1's fragility. And D2's. And all the help I needed when I didn't have it. And all the strength I lost along the way. And the strength I gained. Everything at once, since I became a mother. Reality hasn't settled back into place, it's impossible to follow a discourse without hearing the echo of what is being silenced. I'm worried about how this will affect my writing and what kind of story this will be, this story that's stealing time from my daughters. Writing takes time away from life.

Breastfeeding is natural. So was hunting bison, bare-foot in a loincloth. Now that we have a daughter, I don't even want to buy steak at the grocery store. I want Man to magically become a butcher and I want to carpet our living room with the skins of his kills, because to hunt is in his nature. Would you mind doing that for us, Man? You know how, right? You'll do a great job, because you're a man.

But both times I nursed, my nipples cracked and scabbed while I listened to the voices of mothers scandalized by the perverts who looked at their breasts as they nursed on the metro or in the park. Women with real breasts, real contempt, real disdain. Mothers capable of nursing kids with mouths full of words and teeth. I envy them: I'll never make it that long with my girls. I hear a voice that claims I won't make it because I don't love them as much as those other mothers love their kids. A voice I barely hear, though I swear it speaks to me because I understand exactly what it says. Better mothers than I assure me that my breasts are "naturally made to breastfeed." I don't know. There was a time in which my breasts were naturally made to turn people on. To stick a cock between them, to be groped, to wear something low-cut. For grown men to eat: another kind of food. Isn't the natural thing to remember those other uses, too? Cleavage, nipple, tit, boobs, bowling balls, melons, coconuts, titties, baps, the twins, jugs, udders, bosom, bazongas, knockers, rack, dirty pillows ... all reduced to a pair of mammary glands. Plain old breasts are for feeding, or cancer. I'll do whatever it takes to get my tits back.

Man can't stand the naturalness with which I nurse wherever we find ourselves, in a museum, the park, the metro, a restaurant. He'll never know how much that makes me want him. He demands that I cover up, that I use the muslin blanket, that I don't show anything ... And I tell him that breastfeeding is the most natural thing in the world and I'm aghast and I decry and I take out my breast while fashioning a ridiculous foulard over my shoulder. I'm grateful to Man for understanding that my nipples aren't just nature, that they're also my art and my sex.

The natural thing is for new bodies to seek first times. The natural thing is that I want to give this body that isn't mine to a man who isn't Man. The natural thing is for me to find some stranger who doesn't know any of the women I've been since becoming a mother, a man capable of bringing me back to the woman I was before. A man to take away the pain of losing myself. A man who will never, ever enter our home.

D2 nurses for the last time. It's our last night. "Eat it all up, my love, but don't devour the woman who feeds you."

THIRTY-THREE

ALover

ALover sits at an outside table, waiting for me with his lover's chin and lover's neck and lover's mouth. He has a juicy mouth. He's very handsome, ALover is. We have plans for dinner, maybe just that. Maybe it will be enough.

Before dessert comes, ALover—who is an affectionate man—puts his hand on my thigh and lets me know that any man would want to touch me, that my mother-thighs aren't irrelevant, they can still be a surprise, or a welcome. ALover is a dad, he knows I am a mom. ALover is also happy and overflowing, like me: I would never open this door to a miserable man.

It's very hot the night I meet ALover for dinner, so hot that I have no intention of engaging in any sweaty pursuits; I already feel manhandled by the day and by life. I think I prefer to leave it at a seductive conversation. I'm exhausted, besides, just like the one thousand one hundred and forty-five previous nights. I need to pass out until tomorrow.

Since I became a mother, I shut down every night regardless of the possible options I have before me (a party, a movie, a conversation with Man); there's too much life ahead not to get some sleep. Maybe that's why I'm about to switch into off-mode right here, with ALover sitting across from me in a wicker chair, more awake than me, more focused.

"This heat is terrible," he says. "Restaurants should have showers. I'm soaked."

"That's the first thing I'm going to do when I get home," I reply. "Ice-cold water."

"Or we could take a shower together."

"I don't know, I'm really tired." I appreciate his invitation and would be delighted to accept. It's what we're here for, after all. I explain. "It's just that I'd have to be sensual and obliging with you. I'd have to be really, truly interested in you. And honestly, all I want is to sleep. You don't feel that way?"

ALover laughs. I like ALover because I don't have to be polite or perfect with him, it's not like I'm trying to dupe a complete stranger. He must actually like that about me, if we've made it this far. ALover is also a friend. I've never gone to bed with a complete stranger. He's not bothered by anything I say. In fact, he's amused. And he laughs. I laugh, too. (When a man and woman laugh together, it's always the beginning of something else.)

"I know what you mean. One day, you wake up and it's like the only sex you can imagine after having a family is the sex you had as a teenager. Nothing new to discover. You feel lazy. You feel old. You tell yourself you're still young. And the wheel starts spinning and you're the goddamn rat."

"I'm the mouse fleeing its hole."

"We're in our forties, it's an early midlife thing. We've earned it. We can be tired, we can call each other to have dinner and we can send each other back home. It's all good. But you're not a mouse."

"I'm also not forty yet."

"But you are a very precocious girl."

"Asshole."

"I'm offering a bit of refreshment, that's all," ALover continues. "And in the meantime, maybe I'll get my hands on you. Or maybe I won't. Maybe we just have a glass of wine. Or watch a show."

"That would be the most sensible thing, but I actually think that would be too intimate, unfortunately. At this point, I think we have an *obligation* to sleep together tonight, which is the very reason nothing is going to happen. Am I only one who feels the weight of that 'should'?"

"We all feel it, darling." He raises his glass to me before continuing. "It's like when you finally have a good job: at some point, you get comfortable. And you wish someone would call you in to interview for something new, even when you haven't actually considered—not even for a minute—leaving your position."

"But companies demand innovation. The best employees are constantly learning, up on trends in the market. They're still curious."

"Marriage is an institution, like any other enterprise. And we should treat it as such. Its members should feel obliged to keep themselves up-to-date, or the company gets old and loses its appeal."

ALover is naked. I've picked a good lover. He's a little taller than Man, a little stronger, bigger hands, bigger eyes. Everything a little bigger. But he's not as much of a man as Man. He couldn't be, because he is just ALover.

In the shower, I water myself like a dry plant. It takes a few minutes for me to get soaked through. But he's patient. He waits until I'm completely wet. He checks with his own hands that everything is nice and damp, that I'm ready. Then he opens one of the little hotel shower gels. It smells like citrus, like clementine. And he starts washing me, slowly: my back, arms, neck. He gets on his knees and dedicates himself thoroughly to my legs. He spreads my feet apart on the marble tiles and works his way up, scrubs my hamstrings, his head right between my knees. A little higher and it's his tongue, at last, a different kind of wet.

I think it's a good idea for him to clean me inside, as well.

"I want a glass of wine," I tell ALover while we're still in the shower.

"Better in bed," he replies, unhurried.

ALover isn't after anything. He wants nothing from me, neither one of us requires an ending to this story. In fact, it's the opposite of an ending that we want, it's another glass of wine.

Sex with love serves another purpose. Sex with love is a risk. The risk of letting someone go deeper than anyone else. And—once they're inside—letting them open up all the windows and doors. Sex with love is letting Man find my wounds and stitch them up. And finding his wounds, too. Sex with love doesn't really exist: it is love itself that we are practicing, through sex. Sex that joins us and binds us to the earth and to life. Sex with love binds us. That's why we experience the tension inherent in love like a rope, a rope we cling to, even when we know that it ends in a noose.

Despite this danger, I sleep with Man time after time. And I cling to his love like a port in the storm. Because the seas are raging. And even though I'm there, I know I could be washed away, could drown. But I wouldn't leave that harbor for anything in the world. No one does. We never let go once we find that place, because we sense that haven just might be where we will take shelter our last night on Earth.

ALover turns on the bedside lamp. He puts a glass of wine in one of my hands and a cigarette in the other, tying me up with my vices. I need my mouth to drink and smoke. In other words, I do the same thing I do every night, but with ALover between my legs. ALover's mouth is diligent, hardworking. ALover knows how to open my lips and shut my mouth. ALover is patient, he is kind; he doesn't boast, he isn't proud. I suspect St. Paul slept with ALover before he wrote his Letter to the Corinthians. I don't tell him this joke, but I smile.

There's no poetry in ALover's mouth, just pleasant conversation. No one will be bound or freed or burned in a bonfire tonight. But sometimes, good conversation is the best break. The orange light of dawn will creep up on you but you can continue talking, whispering. You can roll over on the hotel bed, under an enormous window soaring high above Madrid, and say, "I think we forgot to do the other side." And start over, another beginning. And you can be ALover's lover, too, a little later, before you go to work. A little more awake, more generous. Completely clean and grateful.

THIRTY-FOUR

Parenthesis

Six months have passed since my long night with ALover when I wake up in our bed at dawn, on another Sunday morning. I am immensely happy this time, too. But this time my head is clearer and only one desire clouds the room. I want a good woman to approach Man and give him a shower, to clean off the sheen of the exhaustion that stains his shoulders. I can't wipe away all the traces of what weighs on him because his burdens are also mine. Because, after all, I am also Man.

But I doubt it will happen. Man isn't one to step out. I can't expect him to be as responsible with our joint enterprise as I have been; he's very particular about such things. But we're both lucky because I always end up doing what I need to. And thanks to that, we're having a sweet and peaceful morning. We're just here, together. And I don't need to go anywhere else because I want to stay in our home forever. I watch the light filter through the blinds. Light can enter peaceably some days.

I observe Man and I know it will be impossible to grow together without us becoming someone else in our bed, each a stranger to the other.

THIRTY-FIVE

Shall We Take a Selfie?

D1 is in the living room, sitting on the floor by the balcony. Her little arms are crossed over her lap and her head is between her knees. She gives a kick now and then and shakes her head from side to side. No, no, no, no, no.

"Are you mad?" I ask.

"No. I'm saaaad," she replies, drawing out the *a*.

D1 doesn't differentiate between mad and sad. That makes me consider the supposed difference.

Later that night, we're playing on the floor in her room. D2 is sitting with us. We've taken all the building blocks out of their bags and mixed them together, which is unusual. Plastic and wood.

"Mamá, which is more: a whole day, or when spring will be over?"

D1 doesn't differentiate between a whole day and when the spring will end. That makes me consider the supposed difference.

The hardest thing about dealing with kids is living in their world, managing to spend a whole day together there, embracing what is at the heart of a child. On such a day, the spring often passes before the sun even starts to set. I've been trying the entire weekend, trying to inhabit that space, searching for the way to open the door that leads to the sacred territory that is childhood and where, sometimes, an adult slips in to keep them company.

I'm not talking about being near them, taking care of

them, or obeying them. I'm referring to *being* with them, one of those days, one of those moments.

Children perceive time as dissolution and they want us to dissolve with them, but it's complicated. For me, playing with my daughters demands as much concentration as the weekly yoga class where I never quite manage to measure up. My instructor attempts to expand our internal horizons. She asks us to leave everything external, everything that isn't the present moment, at the door; she tries to break down the border between the *I* and the outside. At least for sixty minutes. My daughters simply aren't aware of that border. They live without the ego over their eyes.

That's why playing with them is a form of meditation for me, I think. There is no better master or guide. I'm talking about really playing, which is what I'm attempting to do right now. Put a red square on the green one, set a pink triangle on top, observe it for a few seconds. Make it fall. Now, put a green block on the pink triangle, bring the purple triangle over, search around for the red square and knock the tower down before you find it. Stack orange rectangles one atop the other, only the orange ones this time, as high as only the orange rectangles can go. And wait.

In Buddhism, there is no full attention without compassion. It is understood that mindfulness and loving kindness go hand in hand. In this way, dissolution doesn't consist in dissolving into oneself, ignoring everything else, or letting the mind be blissfully blank. On the contrary. There's a word in Sanskrit that describes this kind of mindfulness: *karuna*. This is the passionate attention a child needs to grow, but it requires determination, rigor, an open mind, and a sort of state of consciousness that is completely incompatible with the pace of my days and my life. For example, I'm thinking about all of this while trying to concentrate on the building blocks with the same focus as the girls, just like in yoga when the instructor demands that I center all my energy and attention on the tip of the long toe on my left foot. And tells me to feel gratitude for that toe and that foot and so on, going over every part of my body. I never manage to make it through the full circuit (foot, ankle, knee, hip, pubis, waist, chest, shoulders, head, nose …) without stopping to think my own thoughts. Like now. It turns out it is impossible to be here completely, as if internal and external didn't exist, as if there wasn't a distinct *I* clamoring inside, as if there wasn't a tomorrow or a kitchen or—of course—a front door leading outside. And then to give thanks from that place, on top of it all.

Which is more? A whole day or when spring will be over?

It turns out I can't do it, I'm not capable. And so instead of focusing on what I should, I allow my arm to act, I let it do what it feels like doing and I watch how it moves my hand to the object I've placed behind my back, out of the girls' sight. And, unpremeditated, my hand picks up the cell phone and takes a picture of what we're doing. This is something that often happens to me when I'm with them: I take pictures and more pictures of the moment that is escaping me.

D2 just took a red square and set it on the top of a tower that will come down on its own, without anyone knocking it over. I can already see it starting to quiver. I'm able to snap a photo right then and capture the image, which I immediately send to MyMother, with a one-word message: *Builders.*

Photos have become my substitute for the moment. My phone's camera roll is glutted with moments I can't quite capture and won't ever look at again. Every once in a while, I think about how I should make an album or a video out of them. These pictures are a kind of proof of life, the evidence that my daughters are mine and that they really have my full attention. That's probably why I'm going to post the photo on Facebook. I won't show her face, just her little hand on the red square and the same description I used with MyMother: #builders. But what exactly are we building?

Photos, social media, the excessive presence of children on social media, the excessive display of parents' love for their children everywhere. These are the ways we tell ourselves—the way I tell myself—that this is our present, that everything is going just fine. There's something incompatible with love in all this, in this way of loving them, I mean. Capture an instant, tag the instant, share it, mention everyone involved … a new form of presence that is anathema to giving attention to the very moment being celebrated.

The red square D2 just put on the top of the orange tower has come tumbling down.

We live in an age of selfies, lists, calendars, Instagram likes, interests. Metric tons of time spent doing things worse than we could do them if only we had a little more time.

None of our towers are standing, now; they've all crumbled and created a colorful cemetery on the rug. I think it's time to pick up … Time to start the bath, supper, teeth, pee, story, nightmare, snuggles …

While Man gets them undressed and starts the bath, I pick up the pieces of the shipwreck scattered throughout the apartment. There's something sad about toys strewn on the floor after an evening of playtime. Toys have a very particular way of being still, as if they feel very alone, paralyzed in their abandonment. Somehow, they remind me of the superficial sadness of when our friends would get drunk at our place, some years ago now, and end up strewn about, helpless after all the fun, passed out on the couch or puking in the bathroom. Could it be the same sadness I feel now, as I vomit in the guest bathroom while the girls splash in the tub on the other side of the wall. Sadness because I realize, as I retch the last bit of bile, that even though love will multiply with each child's arrival, attention to your children is impossible to divide. Loving your children doesn't mean being with them and being with them doesn't necessarily mean inhabiting their space. I think about this and throw up a little more.

THIRTY-SIX

Multiple Choice

My daughters weren't babies anymore when I thought I was dying. D1 was five and D2 two and a half; they'd both made it through daycare, they were both going to school. I had managed to raise two big girls but then I thought I was dying. Something obviously wasn't right. My body wasn't where it should be.

I decided to buy a pregnancy test just so I wouldn't have to tell my life story to a GP. I knew perfectly well what morning sickness was and I knew that, in my case, morning sickness wasn't possible. I planned to see a gynecologist after the test; I hadn't had a pelvic exam since D2 was born. Still, I couldn't help but do a little math. "When was your last period? Recently. When is recently? Three months? Two?" I didn't have the slightest idea when I'd had my last period. It was like asking Man when he had his last goddamn period. It didn't matter. It had never mattered. Because I had always been infertile. Ten years of sex on barren land. That's why the test was absurd. That's why Man didn't know. That's why I waited a whole week, despite the vomiting. I would have sounded crazy if I had asked Man to go to a pharmacy. I was sure I was sick. I started to think about an iron deficiency, then about stress, and then definitely something worse. If felt like I'd boarded a boat at some point and now I couldn't get off it. Endless nausea, body in knots, heaviness invading my red blood cells. Or something worse. I clearly needed to get blood work, but I wanted to take the test before embarking on an odyssey of predictable questions at the clinic. I had conceived before, they would think. But it couldn't be, it was my body invaded by a loss of appetite, a gray exhaustion like a cancer. Or something worse.

I ordered coffee and a toasted baguette with tomato at a café packed with people on their way to work first thing in the morning. Then I went into the bathroom. I hadn't even finished peeing when the lines appeared, accompanied by a knot in my throat I'd never experienced before. I had waited for the results on so many goddamn pregnancy tests, hundreds of drawn-out seconds watching that second line never appear. And now, urine streaming into the toilet bowl in the brown-tiled public restroom, door latched, there they were: two lines. Strong and pink, so intense, almost purple.

My coffee was still steaming on the counter when I came out of the bathroom, as if nothing had happened.

"Don't bother with the toast, I'll just have coffee," I explained to the waitress.

When was your last period? Recently. When is recently?

I paid and, as the waitress handed me ten cents in change, I realized what was about to happen. Because contrary to all expectations, I was going to want, going to dare, going to have an unplanned third child. Man would want to go through with it, even if I didn't. The decision wouldn't be rational, of course, because there is no rational decision without a disguise or lie hiding its face. But it was going to happen, regardless. And at some future moment, I would laugh when telling the café story to a friend, a new baby in my arms.

My heart was a stone on the café counter. And what really happened was that I drank my coffee. And celebrated an arrival. And immediately after, chose a goodbye.

THIRTY-SEVEN

Peter and the Wolf

D1 is performing Sergei Prokofiev's *Peter and the Wolf* with her ballet school tonight. TheNanny and I are seated in red velvet seats in a theater in downtown Madrid, which the school has rented for the occasion. Tickets cost seven euros apiece and the theater is packed with the ballerinas' aunts and uncles, grandparents, and other family members. Man hasn't come. He said he had a meeting that he couldn't move, but the truth is, he doesn't want to be here.

"There is no reason why a five-year-old should be performing anywhere other than in the dance school down the street. Not even if it was in the Compañía Nacional! The right to dance in a performance hall like that must be earned, and I don't understand why they're denying my daughter the right to earn it. We're raising an army of narcissists," he argued when I explained the event.

TheNanny, on the other hand, is delighted with the show. She is the one who braided D1's hair and knotted it in a perfect bun for class every Tuesday and Thursday. She knows how D1 likes to have her tights pulled up, slowly, without pinching her skin. She sewed the pink elastic straps on D1's miniature ballet shoes so her little feet wouldn't slip out.

"Not you, mamá, you hurt me," she said, in the dressing room, as I tried to get her tights on. She had the red lips of a professional dancer.

I don't know why, but the children have had their make-up done by the teachers.

Last week, it was TheNanny who walked to Calle del Arenal to pick up the black leotard D1 is about to debut. She's the one who bought our tickets in the second row and she's the one, obviously, who tells me what is about to happen.

"D1's teacher is a cat. The other classes are ducks and birds, and a professional dancer will be the wolf. The only little boy in D1's class will be Peter. The girls will be dressed as the same animal as their teacher and will do the same dance. The cats come out last," she explains.

That's how I know that D1, who is a cat, isn't on stage yet.

TheNanny lives an ocean away from her country and her family. She's only four years older than me, but her two children are quite a bit older than mine: two boys, eight and eighteen. TheNanny had to say goodbye to her sons at the airport in Cochabamba, Bolivia, when they were two and twelve, the day she had no choice but to come to Spain to take care of other women's children. It would be three years before she saw them again, for just a month, her only vacation. Four years ago, she started visiting them every Christmas. And when she returns to Madrid, it takes between twenty and forty days for her expression and voice to go back to normal. There, in our kitchen, she is a specter back fresh from a near-death experience. TheNanny has seen the white light at the end of the tunnel many times and each time she's chosen to come back to life, take one more step, to bread the cutlets and dry D2's hair while I put on D1's pajamas. With the exception of the days following her visits with her sons, TheNanny is all calm, all smiles. She always manages to be there when Man and I can't, she always has time for them. We are raising my children between the three of us. Since I've chosen to be a working mother, there's only half a woman left of me for our home. Less than half, maybe. That's why we need to add a whole other woman to our family, eight hours Monday through Friday of extra female. But when it's a man working outside the home, the working father's family obligations are never taken up by another man. It doesn't matter how much a man works, how much money he ends up making, how much time he spends away—another man never comes into the picture. But it's different in a woman's case. Every time a female executive becomes established in Spain, a glass ceiling cracks. And, at the same time, another woman (who has recently arrived from a poorer neighborhood or country) registers in the Social Security Office so she can attend to the domestic labor from which the professional woman—i.e. me—will be forever liberated. And collaborate in raising the liberated professional's children (i.e. my daughters). Or be another adult in the house to talk to, like how Man talks to TheNanny, who is always home. During the week, they all eat lunch together in my kitchen.

On stage, Peter—a dark-haired, chubby eight-year-old —has just left the home where he lives with his grandfather in a forest clearing. He left the garden gate open and is chatting with a bird when a duck sees the open gate and decides to walk out for a swim in a nearby pond. The bird and the duck are the teachers, professional dancers capable of controlling every inch of their bodies with animal grace. The stage fills with little ducks, four- and five-year-olds flapping yellow feathers. And now a great flock of black birds appears with grand strides, older girls in Lycra jumpsuits, red crests on their heads. They all wear a black plastic beak over their mouths.

The fathers, mothers, grandparents, and other family members that pack the room photograph every movement in the dark, even though they know the pictures will be blurry, even though the school has informed us that a high-quality DVD of the performance will be available for purchase next Tuesday, so we can all preserve this memory. The best-prepared among us have video cameras, some of which look decidedly professional. There are several tripods set up in the aisle and many mothers kneeling in the front row with their phones ready to go, eyes trained on the screen. It's unclear what is more important: watching our daughters, recording their performance, or making sure they feel the pressure of our expectations loaded on each and every one of their muscles, the expectant tension that—for some reason—so excites us.

As mothers, our excitement is often excessive. Mine is certainly unjustified. It's as if a line was missing from my story, or as if my daughters were secretly, unconsciously, my life's project; how shameful. As if some part of me was willing to follow them around on my knees, phone in hand, taking out-of-focus pictures of them wherever they might decide to go. Given that they are my project, I suspect they will choose well. And a part of me, the sickest part, surely, even goes so far as to think (but never to admit it out loud) that if I do a good job, they will choose well. And so I'll watch them get their diplomas and medals, I'll watch them fall in love with good people, I'll get to see their faces in the college yearbook, I'll help them choose their outfits for every *carnaval*, school dance, concert, and graduation, I'll clap for them at interminable parades, I'll root for them and support them as often as I have to until I extract the most perfect version from all the possible versions of themselves. As the best sculptor shapes and perforates the marble, I will shape their spirits and souls. What a drag.

There comes a point in every fairy tale when the protagonist must question whom to obey, their own ideal self or the *is-ought* (familiar, cultural, social ...). This is-ought always coincides with a rejection of his or her own desires, and it's what I sometimes think we mothers train for. The is-ought that converts our children's desires into what society needs from them. The is-ought I hate in myself when I become another mother overly excited by a children's play, for instance.

Unfortunately, no matter how lovely a figure I sculpt, sooner or later my daughters will destroy it in order to become the sole commanders of their own destinies. What else could they do? And if and when they manage to break what I've built, they will live with resentment toward me for having crippled their desires, resentment burrowed in their hearts like a rat in a hole under a staircase. They will never forgive me for trying to sign my name on a work of art that isn't actually mine. Copyright has always been a delicate subject.

Maybe that's why I want to tell TheNanny that this will never happen to her. That I admire her for having been capable of treating her children not like the subproducts of her creation, but like real human beings. We can separate ourselves from the people we love, but not from our life's work. And that's why in our heart of hearts, none of us mothers here who have paid seven euros a ticket can understand TheNanny. Life and circumstance can explain some things, the disproportionate excitement and glare of the spotlight in the present moment can explain others.

The birds have begun arguing with the ducks, but I have no idea what they're trying to say to each other. Then Peter's cat sneaks out and creeps silently toward the birds. It's Di's teacher, at last, and Peter warns the birds to fly to safety.

My daughter's arrival on stage is announced by the squeezing in my gut. I take a few deep breaths and make a sustained effort to leave my phone in my bag, to not record, to not feel this excitement, to not be so silly, to resist being part of the plot favoring the emergence of a race of ultrasensitive, ultraqualified humans. A legion of narcissists, according to Man, ready only to plug into their phones. Start with exclusive breastfeeding on demand until the age of three, co-sleeping as long as need be, cloth diapers, Waldorf or Montessori daycare, parent-baby swim class, music and movement from age two, theater, non-GMO, organic, or vegan food, and at five, flashes, spotlights, theaters with red velvet seats ... It's one thing to have a child, like TheNanny, and something else to seek outside confirmation that having that child has been worth it. I sometimes think that all my feelings, my efforts and will, should be directed at only one thing: guaranteeing my girls the opportunity to fail. "Every Spaniard has the right to fail," wrote Juan Benet in his single-article Spanish Constitution. And despite being a very masculine declaration, it's a hoop we mothers still haven't learned to jump through.

D2, who has been sitting on my lap and paying close attention to the stage, points to her sister and bounces on my knees. She can also feel just how significant this moment is.

"Yes, that's her," I confirm. "D1 is a dancing cat."

Backstage, the girls have had whiskers painted on their faces and been given headbands with pointy little ears. Long black tails are sewn onto their leotards. D1 laps the back of her hand in a cat-like gesture. She is incredibly, unbearably beautiful, so small and vulnerable. She hops from side to side with her pack while the bird flies off to a tree and the duck swims to the middle of the pond.

The grandfather arrives and scolds Peter for being out in the meadow and warns him that the wolf could come out from the woods. Peter claims he isn't afraid, that he's very brave and can trap the wolf, or so I understand from his gestures. The grandfather pulls him by the ear back inside the house and shuts the door. A moment later, a gorgeous male dancer, 5' 10" with a ferocious, bare chest, enters the scene. The teacher-bird and teacher-cat climb to safety in a wooden tree. The teacher-duck is left face-to-face with the wolf. Meanwhile, all the little ballerinas circle around to admire the teachers' final dance in which the wolf will catch and eat the duck before the audience's eyes. Peter, the chubby boy, witnesses the scene from behind a crack in the door, while D2 covers her eyes and peeks at the heightened drama through the crack between her fingers. TheNanny is laughing like a child. She is truly amused by what is happening up on stage. Now the girls all run around, imitating their teachers, each little wolf with its own little duck. The ruffled mess of duck feathers, strewn in the gray wolves' attack, the dancing tails, all those little ducks, devoured, all the little cats up on little chairs converted into leafy trees, thanks to cardboard branches sprouting from the seatbacks. The ballerinas run back and forth across the stage, imitating the teachers' movements, looking for their parents in the darkness of the seating area. D1 doesn't look out at us, she's as focused as a samurai. Right now, I don't think anyone could convince her that she isn't a cat. The big gray wolf takes a ferocious swipe at the audience with his claw, yellow feather stuck between his lips, and I burst into tears while TheNanny claps and cheers, dying of laughter.

Childhood is the perfect mix of two contradictory elements: absolute power and maximum vulnerability.

Children are so obviously fragile that we constantly make them aware of their power, time and again. This is being a parent. Because they experience a world that doesn't fit in their hands. That's why kids need manga and Power Rangers and Superwoman and the Goonies and *Stranger Things*. To remember that inside every child pulses a great power. And from the combination of these two elements springs that feeling—the soul-state, I'd even say—that childhood bestows on every human being who has ever had one. That ambivalence is what makes us grow.

This bittersweet inchoateness is the reason I can't stop crying when I see all those girls on the stage, so powerful, authentic belles of the ball, of all the balls. They take little bows for the audience and they really do feel strong, yet I can't help but cry for their fragility, for all that's to come, for all they times they'll get hurt. For how hard it will be to remind them that they are fragile, too, after such a show. I cry because all you have to do is remove one of the elements to rob them of their childhood. A child soldier doesn't have a childhood, and neither does a spoiled little girl. Ambivalence. Sometimes I think that we have renounced raising children, that what we want instead are young gods, magnificent and powerful beings.

I will not rob my daughters of their childhood, I make that promise now. Write it again, a hundred times, I demand of myself. I'm still in my seat, praying they keep the house lights down. TheNanny will be in for a shock if she sees me like this, a mess of tears. I don't know if she would understand. I will not rob my daughters of their childhood. I will not rob my daughters of their childhood. I will not rob my daughters of their childhood. Ambivalence. I'm a child crying in the velvet seat. I'm

pregnant and I am the most fragile and the most powerful being on Earth. I cry for the child I am. And for the
wolf. And the duck. Thank god D1 got to be a cat, I sigh.
And I dry my eyes and run to hug her.

THIRTY-EIGHT

Termination

The first decision I made after I aborted what would have been my third child was to line my upper eyelid, not just the bottom. Forty years old and incapable of drawing the damn line on my top lid, not with regular eyeliner and certainly not with gel. You are not a fully grown woman if you can't line your eyes.

At the clinic, they're asking me a lot of questions. Questions that will give me away.

"Are you using some form of birth control?"

"No."

"Is someone forcing you to make this decision?"

"No."

"Would your partner support you if you chose to continue this pregnancy?"

"Yes."

"Do you have children?"

"Yes."

"Ages?"

"Five and two and a half."

"Marital status?"

"Married."

"Previous abortions?"

"No."

"Would you have the resources to care for this child?"

"Yes."

"Have you been sleeping okay since you found out you are pregnant?"

"Yes."

"What do you imagine having this baby would be like?"

"I lost several implanted embryos during IVF. It's clinically premature to talk about a baby at six weeks of gestation, Doctor. There is no baby."

"Are you able to imagine how your life would be with three children in the event that you carried this pregnancy to term?"

I don't answer that one. It's hard for me to imagine how it would be to raise I child I don't want to have. That's part of the reason I'm here, because I'm not prepared to imagine it.

"Does your partner agree with this decision?"

"Yes."

Man agrees, but I ask him to stay in the waiting room, given that his opinion has no bearing on the psychiatrist's report. It is critical I confirm that I am making a free and conscious choice before they can do the procedure. It's an evaluation of the woman's will. Man has a voice, but no vote. At least not here, not in this room. Other couples have gone in together, as if they were making the decision between them, when they both know that's not the case. I ask Man to wait for me outside. Because children might belong to both parents but an abortion belongs exclusively to the mother. The right is ours alone, we don't need a father to abort. Regardless of who we have next to us, we always abort alone. That's why I've asked Man to come to the clinic. Because of how terribly alone I'm going to feel. Man knows it. And he keeps still. Quiet. As steady and as worn as an ancient Doric column: something I can cling to, though it's on the verge of crumbling. I would only have to press. But I don't.

Man doesn't look at me or hold my hand or make sad little faces like the ones a kid in his early thirties with fake New Balance sneakers is making in the chair opposite me. He's stroking a woman's hair. She's going to have an abortion, too. The kid's gesture looks like an imitation, something he saw in a movie. This couple makes me very sad.

There are a lot of us at the clinic the morning of my abortion: ten women, at least, join me in the waiting room during the half hour I'm there. The clinic is open all day. They don't close for lunch. Every year, between 90,000 and 100,000 women have abortions in Spain. Ninety percent of those abortions are carried out according to the express wish of the future mother. The remaining ten percent result from serious risk to the mother or fetus. A quarter of all pregnancies in the world end in abortion. There are many of us. I don't know why we feel so alone.

The psychiatrist gives my testimony the green light. If she hadn't, I would have had to bring home a pile of documentation about what an abortion entails, economic assistance available to raise the child, and things like that. I could then have an abortion three days post-receipt of that information, without a psychiatric evaluation. According to the law.

I sign all the papers that will lead to the procedure. I tell myself that I'm going to have something to eat when it's all over. A slice of potato omelet and a Coke, for example. Following medical protocol, I haven't eaten in fourteen hours.

Another woman is with me in the room where they have me waiting to be called. She isn't Spanish, and she's moaning softly. The procedure costs 354 euros with local anesthesia and 454 with sedation, a kind of general anes-

·

thesia that doesn't require intubation. With the most expensive option, a woman breathes on her own the whole time but enjoys the same benefits of general anesthesia: analgesia, sleep, and most importantly, amnesia, elimination of any memory of what occurs under sedation. I choose the more expensive option and I know I won't feel pain. Six weeks gestation. The blink of an eye. They perform abortions up to the twenty-second week here. But we fear the memory more than pain. Fortunately, I can pay extra for the amnesia.

I have always defended other women's abortion rights. I fought for that right, protested for it, signed petitions, bought purple T-shirts. It was a right other women needed and deserved. An abortion was something that I simply would never have to have. And in fact, it was something I would never, ever do, because I understood better than anybody the miracle it took to conceive, because I had heard the heartbeat of a whale in my belly. I knew that I would never do it. NEVER. Never, never would I snuff out that heartbeat. But suddenly, violently, a life was unfurling before me, against me, prepared to live in spite of me, determined to be born without permission or desire. And there was a pain in my chest and that heat and that way of being pregnant in a café on a Monday morning, unable to imagine anything worse or anything better. Because I knew that my pregnancy was a good thing. And I knew very well what kind of woman I was.

The nurse asks me to disrobe completely and sit down on the cot in one of those humiliating johnnies that leave your ass exposed. Then she takes my blood. Before she leaves the room, she points to three drops of blood on the sheet and explains that they escaped during the blood draw.

"Don't worry, that's your blood on the sheet," she says. "They'll be right in for you."

The clinic is old but everything is clean, though a slight sense that it might not be hovers in the air. Many of the aides are immigrants, as are many of the patients. My aide is blonde and blue-eyed. On the website, they claim to be able to treat patients in any language. I'm not wearing a watch, but I wait on the cot a long time. I'm cold.

I haven't seen the other woman who had been waiting in the room with me for some time. The plastic curtains have been drawn between us. Maybe they've already taken her in for the procedure. I don't hear her moaning or sighing.

The curtains separate me from something, or conceal it from me. There are gray letters printed on them, lots of letters that give the impression of a big bowl of alphabet soup. They're shower curtains, actually, which is odd. Shower curtains straight out of some student apartment. In the enormous alphabet soup that separates me from the other women, there are four words written and circled in a thick line. *Taxi. Hotel. Spot. Bonita.* Words that turn to stone before my eyes, a coded message. The only words I could eat at a time like this.

We don't know what to do after the procedure. We're not upset, really, we aren't those kinds of people. We want to throw the first fistful of dirt on this moment, bury it under the weight of the quotidian. But there are still two hours before we have to pick the girls up from school. We don't have anywhere to go on this unforeseen workday morning in Madrid, a city where people don't wander, where everyone is on their way someplace, moving fast, because everyone has it all figured out. I think this is why I've always wanted to live here: to have somewhere to be running to every day, every hour. To never have to wander again.

Man says he'd like to buy himself a vest. Seasonal sales have started. We go to a mall near the school. There are so many lights, so many people, so many escalators going up and down, so few windows. I'm wearing a pad. I don't know if I've started to bleed yet. It doesn't hurt, just the occasional, soft pinch. I question whether it's a shadow of pain or of guilt, but it's a shadow that won't leave me for another month. A shadow that will only go out for a walk, and come back. Like Peter Pan's. The shadow faces me head-on every time I go out to meet it.

THIRTY-NINE

Mother's Day

There is a woman in a cave. This is one thing I'm sure of. The woman is taking care of many babies, all the babies. The babies are noisy and most of them are seated and strapped in their high chairs, complete with the five-point harness. Here and there, a calm baby sits in a stroller, and the littlest ones stick their hands out between the bars of the cribs. All the babies are set down or secured in such a way that they can only look at the back wall of the cave. Just behind them, there is a wall with a hallway and, further down, a fire and the entrance to the cave which opens to the outside. The woman walks the hallway (I'd swear she's the mother of them all), day and night, carrying objects whose shadows are projected on the wall in the firelight for the babies to see.

Every once in a while, in a great while, the woman (the mother) is freed from her chores and makes it outside. She sees reality and discovers how things really are; the woman is the only one who sees a tree instead of the tree's shadow.

Plato devised this allegory to explain human beings' relationship to knowledge, though in the original Greek there weren't women or children, just captive men. And since that foundational story, the history of knowledge has basically been an abstract dialogue between males. But Plato's myth is something like pearls are to teeth, a perfect image that illustrates another reality. We are those teeth, we women who didn't make it into any history of ideas, we're the ones who bite the apple. And a mouth without teeth doesn't bite, it just swallows. We're all tired of swallowing. The genocide of the feminine is the reason we choke on life.

So we have a mother, that's me, with D1 and D2, inside a cave. It's my responsibility to go about projecting objects, colors, and tastes on the wall of our house. And that's exactly what I do.

"What does the doggie say? What does the donkey say?" I ask my daughters, girl prisoners, as I project images of animals in a storybook.

"To-ma-*toe*," I say as they eat.

And I hold up the red fruit.

"Chair, mermaid, love," I say.

And then I point: shadow, shadow, shadow.

We never stop pointing to shadows, we mothers. Often, toys facilitate our work. It isn't always possible for a woman to leave her cave in order to find the concept she's looking for, but in this we've advanced from Plato to the smartphone. Any mother has the toy shadows for almost any idea, concept, or living thing at her disposal. In addition to mobile apps, of course. Going outside is no longer necessary, neither is lighting a fire, or even having a house or cave. It's enough to have a phone. Shadows project in all directions and distance us from reality more than ever.

And so our future is unavoidably linked to which kind of mother lives in each house. Because the keeper of the shadows also holds the key to freedom in her apron pocket, assuming there's any light left beyond the walls of the cave.

Unfortunately, everyone knows how this myth ends. It turns out that if the person who knows the outside world (me, the mother) attempts to liberate those still living in shadows, they will laugh at her, at first. But if she insists (if I endeavor to bring my girls toward the light), they'll decide to kill her.

This is why the journey toward truth is always so terrifying. There it is written and that's how we mothers remember it, scared to death. What to do then, with our chubby little prisoners? What will I do with my daughters when the time comes? Encourage them to leave, or bite off their big toes in our warm cave? At the moment, what I like most is to shut ourselves up inside the house and play and make shadow puppets on the wall. Inside, no one watches us, no one touches us, and everything that is outside and real can keep waiting because, for the moment, we don't want it.

But deep down I know that my pups, sooner or later, will bite off my hand if I don't take them for a walk. We're not raising puppies, we're raising wolves, creatures as wild as we are. And who hasn't ripped the arm off their own mother?

I don't remember the first time I said it to MyMother, but I couldn't have been more than twelve. After that, resentment kept growing rampantly between us.

"Don't you get that it's my life?" An arrow shot straight at MyMother's forehead. A perfect mark between her thin, blond brows.

From that day forward.

One day: "I know you wouldn't do it like this, but it's my life." And another: "Can't you ever stop meddling?" One month: "I'm thirty-six years old. This is my house and I'll do things my way." And another: "Will you ever understand that I'm not you? Can't you see that I don't even want to be like you?" One year: "Well, maybe I do know what I'm doing and I choose to do the opposite of what you would." And another: "I understand you're disappointed in me, but this is what I've chosen." And another: "Have you ever asked yourself if I'm disappointed by how *you* do things?"

I've never had to tell another human being that I'm in charge of my own life more times than I've had to tell MyMother. And I finally understand that if I can do that, it's only because she took me by the hand and led me outside her cave. She let me leave, she freed me. And how do I repay her? By laughing at her or killing her with my own two hands if necessary (and some days I actually think it's about to become necessary), because that's how it's written. Unfortunately for me, knowledge is circular, it turns like a wheel. And I have the feeling all the arrows I've let fly will stick in my own forehead sooner or later, loosed by my daughters. But wait, what is all this? Just how big a trap is motherhood? Big enough for a bird, an elephant, a whale, the whole world.

When they are grown at last, free and independent women, when I walk outside with them and the three of us are naked before all the truth and all the beauty of this world, won't I still hold even a little preferred stock in their lives? What do they plan to do with all the time and love I've given them?

I have spread my dreams under your feet;
tread softly because you tread on my dreams

I stencil W.B. Yeats's lines on the kitchen wall and make sure they'll mark it forever. I paint each letter angrily, as if I were smashing all the plates in the house one by one. And the wineglasses. The nice wineglasses someone gave us at Christmas. One by one. To hell with it all.

Granted, it will be their life to choose but this hasn't stopped me from wanting to do everything for them, because their independence is a gift we will have to open together, sooner or later. Granted, I'm writing this book instead of clocking hours at the park. Granted, I don't plan on blaming them for what I didn't do while they were growing up because I don't expect any reward other than our present time together. Granted, I still have my job and all the things that were important to me before they came. Granted, my head is full of words. But what happens when they're free to make their own decisions? When they hurt themselves, when they fall in love with someone who hurts them, when they literally fall in love with pain, when they lack willpower, when they're frivolous, when they're bad, when they're the ones who hurt others, when they choose to destroy their bodies, when they'll accept anything. When they forget their mother.

If this is the treat, it almost makes more sense to choose the trick. I think I prefer being one of those mothers who don't make trouble for themselves, just as bountiful and respected as the rest. Mothers who imprison their children in their own way of thinking and that's the end of it. Those mothers sit in their living room or their kitchen (or garden or villa, if the budget permits) and dedicate their entire lives to convincing their children that the mother is the only thing that's real. And so on and so forth until the mother is both queen and prisoner and the child only feels safe in the shadows of the maternal home or childhood.

Trick or treat. Hard to know which is the best way to awaken our children's desire for light: confinement or generosity. Personally, I don't think it matters. Children always do what they can to escape. But some prisons really are perfect, especially mental ones.

Now I know. Real mothers have watched their children leave, they've said goodbye to them out in the light of the real world, they've accepted that they have nothing left to do with them now. And they've smiled. Seriously. They've smiled. So, in the best of cases, I still have a long way—a really long way—to go before I'm a mother. Giving birth isn't enough. Love and breast and time and all the rest aren't enough. Who cares about any of that? *Mother* is the one who gets you out of the cave, and for this we need men who aren't obsessed with filling it with more and more stuff. Sweep aside your money and your power and help us get out, papá. Find the woman inside you, papá, because we need her in this house. In every house, papá.

The day my daughters kill me hasn't come yet, lucky for me. But it will. God closes doors and he shuts windows, too. And in the end, motherhood—like knowledge—is an imagined trip toward life or death.

I have two daughters. I'm about to finish a book about motherhood and at the end of this trip there's nothing but a filthy wall to slam into, headfirst. Either that, or I can start wiping off the dirt. I fear another woman should have written this story, a real mother. Mine, for example. Because one isn't a real mother until her children have bid her farewell, until they leave her and leave the cave and are with life instead. A woman (or man) isn't a mother until they've set a human being free on this earth and released them into the light where everything can be good and true and beautiful. When that day comes—the luminous moment an individual gains their freedom—you will hear the sound of their mother's heart, which has broken.

So now, all that's left to hope is that everything goes okay and that—one day—it will be my heart that shatters into pieces.

Acknowledgments

First and foremost, I want to thank three women who were inspiration and encouragement for this book. Without them, it wouldn't have happened. To Rosa Montero, motivation and premonition for this novel, and my support during the hardest years when writing seemed like a luxury it was high time to give up. To Lara Moreno, for believing in this story as if it were her own. Or better yet, as if it were all of ours. And for reading it and caring for it as if it were a friend's. And to María Sendagorta, for always reading from a different perspective, for her way of underlining and questioning my manuscripts, and for helping me, once again, to the very end.

Thank you to Doctor Javier Santisteban, the man who helped me give birth to my daughters. From him, I learned the serious, delicate care that life deserves, beyond where words can reach. In this sense, I have tried to make my way of writing about life in this book emulate his way of working with it.

Thank you from the bottom of my heart to Claudio López de Lamadrid for making this newcomer feel at home. This book wouldn't exist if it weren't for his confidence in me.

And to Albert Puigdueta for all his help. For reading and reading again, with passionate detail and for putting himself time and time again in another's skin.

To the Fundación Valparaíso, for welcoming the writing of a first draft, one July that would change everything. A special thank you to Beatrice Beckett, whom I had the pleasure of meeting personally. She and her husband, Paul Beckett, have been the support and sustenance of many.

To the Escuela Contemporánea de Humanidades de Madrid, for being a refuge for thought in the midst of the cold. And to my seminar colleagues, each one of you, for being refuge for me.

Lastly, I thank Alejandro Gándara, who asked expressly not to appear in these acknowledgments. Writer and mentor to writers, whom I will limit myself to thanking "only" for his invaluable domestic help. Thank you for making me believe that food grows in the refrigerator. And that, at least in ours, it grows already cooked. But above all, thank you for helping me free that mental space that neither books nor teachers can open, only love.

KATIE WHITTEMORE translates from the Spanish. She is the translator of *Four by Four* (Open Letter Books, 2020) by Sara Mesa, and her work has appeared in *Two Lines*, *The Arkansas International*, *The Common Online*, *Gulf Coast Magazine Online*, *The Brooklyn Rail*, and *InTranslation*. Current projects include novels by Spanish authors Sara Mesa, Javier Serena, and Aliocha Coll (for Open Letter Books), and Aroa Moreno Durán (for Tinder Press). She lives in Valencia, Spain.

On the Design

As book design is an integral part of the reading experience, we would like to acknowledge the work of those who shaped the form in which the story is housed.

Tessa van der Waals (Netherlands) is responsible for the cover design, cover typography, and art direction of all World Editions books. She works in the internationally renowned tradition of Dutch Design. Her bright and powerful visual aesthetic maintains a harmony between image and typography and captures the unique atmosphere of each book. She works closely with internationally celebrated photographers, artists, and letter designers. Her work has frequently been awarded prizes for Best Dutch Book Design.

The image on the cover comes from an advertisement for Craven A cigarettes, which was inserted in the Christmas Issue of the British weekly magazine *The Illustrated Sporting and Dramatic News* in 1939. The campaign's slogan was: "Will Not Affect Your Throat." Like many ads in the years between the two world wars, this one specifically targeted women, who were the growing market, and tried to associate smoking with sophisticated urban taste. The cigarette has been digitally removed from the photograph leaving the image of a daydreaming woman staring out of the frame.

The cover has been edited by lithographer Bert van der Horst of BFC Graphics (Netherlands).

Suzan Beijer (Netherlands) is responsible for the typography and careful interior book design of all World Editions titles.

The text on the inside covers and the press quotes are set in Circular, designed by Laurenz Brunner (Switzerland) and published by Swiss type foundry Lineto.

All World Editions books are set in the typeface Dolly, specifically designed for book typography. Dolly creates a warm page image perfect for an enjoyable reading experience. This typeface is designed by Underware, a European collective formed by Bas Jacobs (Netherlands), Akiem Helmling (Germany), and Sami Kortemäki (Finland). Underware are also the creators of the World Editions logo, which meets the design requirement that "a strong shape can always be drawn with a toe in the sand."